# BOYS *and* GIRLS *of* BOOKLAND

# BOYS AND GIRLS OF BOOKLAND

By

NORA ARCHIBALD SMITH

Illustrated in Color by

## JESSIE WILLCOX SMITH

DERRYDALE BOOKS

NEW YORK

Copyright © 1988 by OBC, Inc.

This 1988 edition is published by Derrydale Books,
distributed by Crown Publishers, Inc., 225 Park Avenue South,
New York, New York 10003.

Printed and bound in the United States of America

Library of Congress Cataloging-in-Publication Data

Smith, Nora Archibald, 1859–1934.
Boys and girls of bookland.

Summary: Presents condensed versions of eleven
classics, including "David Copperfield," "Little Women,"
"Alice in Wonderland," "Heidi," and
"Rebecca of Sunnybrook Farm."
1. Children's stories. [1. Short stories]
I. Smith, Jessie Willcox, 1863–1935, ill. II. Title.
PZ5.S66Bo 1988    [Fic]      87–36517
ISBN 0–517–66206–X

h g f e d c b a

# CONTENTS

# LIST OF COLOR PLATES

# FOREWORD

Some of the most beloved characters in children's literature spring to life in the pages of *Boys and Girls of Bookland*. These eleven retellings by Nora Archibald Smith, first published in the first quarter of this century, acquaint young readers with classics they will want to read later in the original. The acquaintance is established in the most natural way: through the fictional boys and girls who live in these books. It is the identification with, and empathy for, character that causes a book to resonate inside us —to enlighten, give pleasure, become immortal.

Author Smith has evident appreciation for her subjects, and, with a light-handed, at times humorous approach, she tells who the characters are, where and how they live, and what happens to them. Some original dialogue is woven in, to enhance the sense of character and atmosphere. Settings are important, and there is a great variety here: from the gray, dismal London of "Tiny Tim" and "Little Nell" to the bright, icy canals of "Hans Brinker"; from the flower-strewn alpine meadows of "Heidi" to the lush tropical jungle of "Mowgli." We are always given a sense of the character in his or her environment. As real children are sensitive to their surroundings, and thirst after the new and exotic, they will enjoy discovering the interesting terrain each story offers.

One of the strengths of these retellings is a sense of restraint: Smith does not divulge too much about a book, but just enough to intrigue and invite the reader inside it. Indeed, the love of books and of reading is shared by the characters themselves: David Copperfield, the March girls, the Little Lame Prince, and others learn early on the delights to be found in literature.

At moments, the author's style may seem somewhat stylized or flowery, but this can be understood in the context of her time. It is only recently that realism and minimalism have become standards; in the early part of this century, authors tended toward romanticization and hyperbole. There was also a tendency toward moral instruction, especially the advocacy of "proper" behavior. Of course, what was considered proper for boys was *not* considered proper for girls. Girls were groomed "to warn, to comfort, and command" within the relatively protected world of the home, while boys were encouraged toward more worldly pursuits. On the other hand, there were exceptions: Jo March decides to become a writer and, through hard work, realizes success.

Success over adversity is an important theme in children's literature, and this book is filled with characters whose situations improve through their own efforts and sacrifices. Hans Brinker persists in asking a famous surgeon to save his father, despite his family's poverty. Mowgli defends the old wolf, Akela, against Shere Khan, the tiger, gaining the eternal loyalty of his jungle friends. And Little Nell leads her grandfather away from their squalid life in London to make a new start in the countryside. Childhood is filled with difficulties and challenges; the courage and resourcefulness of these and other characters strike a responsive chord in young readers.

Jessie Willcox Smith provided luminous color illustrations for this anthology which convey the essence of its young heroes and heroines. They are lovingly drawn; their faces express a sensitivity and spirit that is vibrant, if idealized. But it is idealization in the sense of capturing a distilled quality of the real child: a wishful, watchful, *open* innocence. We can imagine these children taking on whatever difficulties life presents them.

The artist herself knew adversity. At the time when she began to illustrate magazines and children's books, in the late nineteenth century, few female artists had achieved commercial success. Smith's upbringing in rigid Victorian Philadelphia society had taught her that a woman's role was as a wife and mother. Her first job, as a kindergarten teacher, was short-lived. The decision to become an illustrator was a very brave and independent move. Later, Smith's artistic talents and ambitions were encouraged, notably by her mentor, Howard Pyle, and Smith was able to achieve a popular and financial success surpassing that of any other female artist prior to, or during, her own time.

One of Smith's observations about Pyle's teaching offers an interesting perspective on her work for this book:

There was your story, and you knew your characters, and you imagined what they were doing, and in consequence you were bound to get the right composition because you lived these things . . . *

Evidently, the artist applied this philosophy to her own work with telling results. In each illustration, the figures are generally seen in motion within a dynamic environment, often out-of-doors. One surely has the sense that the artist understood and, in some measure, "lived" her subjects.

In her opening to "David Copperfield," the author calls David "as real a boy as ever walked on two feet, although his life was spent within the covers of a book." This is true of all fine characters in literature, though, more often than not, they walk right off the page and into our lives. Their hopes, loves, fears, struggles, aspirations, and adventures become our concerns, and we feel the pull of regret on approaching the end of each story. This first acquaintance with Jo and Meg, Tiny Tim, Alice, the Little Lame Prince, Mowgli, and other wonderful children will launch lasting relationships with the original classics.

ELLEN DREYER

BROOKLYN, NEW YORK
1988

EDITORIAL NOTE

*In several instances the author converts foreign currencies into U.S. dollar amounts. These monetary conversions reflect the exchange rates at the time of her writing and do not reflect today's rates of exchange.*

*Jessie Willcox Smith*, by S. Michael Schnessel. New York: Thomas Y. Crowell, n.d.

# DAVID COPPERFIELD

AVID COPPERFIELD, as real a boy as ever walked on two feet, although his life was spent within the covers of a book, was born in a quaint old house in England, called Blunderstone Rookery, and something that might be called a misfortune happened to him on his very first birthday. His great-aunt, Miss Betsey Trotwood, called at his home on that date, expecting that the new baby would be a girl, and with that idea in mind she had a name selected for her and plans made for her education.

When Miss Trotwood heard that, instead of being aunt to a girl made of sugar and spice and all that's nice, she was merely aunt to a boy, compounded, as we all know, of snips and snails and puppy-dogs' tails, she was justly indignant, and she tied on her bonnet very hard, pinned on her shawl very tight, and left the house at once, never to return to it. She did return to the story, as I might as well say now—but that was a long time afterwards.

Little David's father had died before he was born, and so there was only his beautiful young mother to love him and care for him. His nurse's name was Peggotty, a stiff and prickly name, as prickly as a chestnut-bur, and like the chestnut was Peggotty; and as sound and sweet inside. Clinging to her work-worn finger, as rough as a pocket nutmeg-grater, David took his first steps in front of the evening fire, and in time could run on rapid feet from her knee to his mother's arms.

Those were happy times, by and by, when he could sit in his little chair by the flickering flames and hear his mother tell him stories, while Peggotty stitched away on the other side of the hearth.

Happy, too, those evenings when his mother danced with him in the twilight, just the two of them, with her bright eyes dancing to the measure, her bright cheeks flushing, and her long, bright curls keeping time. Happier, still, the hour when tired and sleepy he leaned his head upon her shoulder and her soft hair falling over his cheek felt like the touch of an angel's wing.

There was a wonderful occasion, later on, when David had grown wise and learned and was reading to Peggotty a traveler's tale about some beasts which she understood to be called "crorkindills." While he was spelling out what the book told him of their ferocity, Peggotty suddenly interrupted him to inquire if he would like to go on a visit with her to her brother's house in Yarmouth, a seaside town not far away. David had never been on any journey farther than the boundaries of his own village, and was enchanted with the idea as soon as he learned that his mother approved and would not be lonely in his absence. The journey was made in an old-time way—in which none of you boys and girls will ever travel—in a carrier's cart with a slow and plodding horse to draw it, and Barkis, the slow and plodding carrier to drive. Bundles were delivered along the way, and passengers taken up and dropped, and when at last the travelers smelled the sea and found Peggotty's nephew, Ham, waiting to meet them, how exciting were the town and the shops and the fishy-smelling streets! Threading these streets, at last they came upon the flats, and there was the house where David was to visit; but, wonder of all wonders, it was not an ordinary dwelling at all, but a black barge or boat drawn up safe and sound on the sand out of the reach of old ocean!

"If it had been Aladdin's palace, roc's egg and all," says David in the book about him, "I could not have been more charmed with the romantic idea of living in it.

"There was a delightful door cut in the side, and it was roofed in, and there were little windows in it; but the wonderful charm of it was that it was a real boat which had no doubt been upon the water hundreds of times, and which had never been intended to be lived in on dry land. That was the captivation of it."

If it had ever been meant to be lived in, David might have thought it small, or inconvenient, or lonely; but never having been designed for any such use, it became a perfect abode.

Inside it was beautifully clean, with everything tucked away in a small space, as it is on board ship, with hooks in the beams of the ceiling to hang hammocks from, with lockers and boxes to sit on and eke out the chairs, and the completest bedroom ever seen in the stern of the vessel for Davy, with a little window and a little looking-glass framed in oyster shells, a little bed, and a nosegay of seaweed in a blue mug on the table.

When Davy found out that there was a playmate for him, too, in this Noah's Ark of a house, a fair-haired, blue-eyed little girl named Emily— "Little Em'ly" they called her—his joy was great indeed, and all he wanted in the world was to cry, "Heave ho! my hearties! Hoist up the anchor!" and to sail away on the raging main with all on board.

But as the anchor had long ago disappeared, and there seemed to be no "hearties" to man the bark, David concluded to stay on land and enjoy the hospitality of Peggotty's brother, who was a "hairy, seafaring man with a good-natured face." A kind man, an honest man, a friendly man was the brother, and his quaint abode sheltered his nephew Ham whose father was "drowndead," Little Em'ly, her father also "drowndead," and Missis Gummidge, his melancholy housekeeper, whose husband, alas! was "drowndead," too.

David's happy days of childhood were not many; but those on Yarmouth flats with Little Em'ly, sailing boats, picking up shells and pebbles on the beach, sitting on a locker in the evening by the fire while the fierce wind howled out at sea, were among the happiest of all. But they were soon over, as indeed was the happiness itself for many a long day, and the time came for Barkis, the carrier, and the return to Blunderstone Rookery.

Glad as his mother was to see her boy again, there had been changes in the family since David left that soon made it best for him to be sent away to boarding-school, and on a cold gray morning with a dull sky threatening rain, the little boy hugged and kissed his dear mother many, many times, and again climbed into the carrier's cart, his box of clothing beside him, and set off on his long journey to Salem House, near London.

They had gone only about half a mile, and David's handkerchief was quite wet with tears, when Barkis stopped short and through the roadside hedge burst Peggotty. She climbed into the cart, squeezed and squeezed her nursling so hard that nearly all the buttons flew off the back of her gown, gave him a bag of cakes and a small purse of money, climbed down again and disappeared, red-eyed and sobbing.

This was a melancholy beginning to a long journey; but by and by David remembered that none of the heroes in his favorite books had ever cried, so far as he could remember and Barkis offering to spread the wet handkerchief on the horse's back to dry, the two fell into conversation. Barkis made many inquiries about Peggotty—whether she had any "sweethearts," whether she made all the "apple parsties" and did all the cooking —and, receiving encouraging replies, begged David to say when he was next writing to her that "Barkis was willin'."

David had not the least idea what this message meant, but perhaps you, who are older and wiser, can guess. At all events, David did as he was told, and when he reached his first stopping-place procured a sheet of paper and an inkstand and wrote a note to Peggotty, which ran thus:

"My dear Peggotty: I have come here safe. Barkis is willing. My love to Mama. Yours affectionately. P. S. He says he particularly wants you to know BARKIS IS WILLING."

Salem House, under its Head Master, Mr. Creakle, was a boarding-school where boys were taught as little and feruled and caned as much as could possibly be managed in the hours of the day, and David was very miserable there, lonely, and homesick, and forsaken. He made friends with some of the masters and with many of the boys; but his best and dearest among his companions were Tommy Traddles and James Steerforth. Tommy Traddles, in a sky-blue suit so tight that it made his arms and legs look like German sausages or roly-poly puddings, was the merriest and most miserable of all the boys. He was always being caned—was caned every day of the first half-year except one holiday, Monday, when he was only feruled on both hands—was always going to write his uncle about it and never did. He would lay his head on the desk afterward for a while, then cheer up again, begin to laugh and to draw skeletons all over his slate before his eyes were dry. He had an extraordinary facility in drawing these skeletons, and once when he was imprisoned in the dormitory for many hours as a punishment, he came out "with a whole churchyard full of skeletons swarming all over his Latin Dictionary."

Steerforth, older, more experienced, more considered and more able than the other boys, was the hero of the school; and he watched over and protected little David and made his way as easy for him as he could. He discovered one day that his charge had read many books and could tell stories from them, and he established a series of "Arabian Nights' Entertainments" in the dormitory where, all sitting around him in the dark, David recounted the histories of "Roderick Random," "Peregrine Pickle," "Humphry Clinker,"

"Tom Jones," "The Vicar of Wakefield," "Don Quixote," "Gil Blas," and "Robinson Crusoe."

At last, while still at Salem House, came David's tenth birthday—a foggy, frosty, ghostly day, when the poor child was told that his beloved young mother was dead, and that now he was quite alone in the world. When the funeral and all the last sad arrangements were over, it was decided that the boy, now motherless, fatherless, friendless, and penniless, should be sent to London to the firm of Murdstone and Grinby, in the wine trade, and should there do what he could to earn his eating and drinking and pocket money. His lodging at first was to be paid for him, and in a much-worn little white hat with a black crape around it for his mother, a black jacket and a pair of hard, stiff corduroy trousers, David set out in a post-chaise to begin his fight with the world.

Murdstone and Grinby's warehouse was at the waterside, an old and dirty building with decaying roofs and staircases, and there, day after day, David, with three or four companions, looked over, rinsed, washed, and labeled empty bottles. He lodged with Mr. and Mrs. Micawber, a kindly couple, who were always in debt, and who were always sending him to the pawnbrokers to get money on the family silver, and always expecting something to "turn up," which would get them out of difficulties. David's wages were six shillings a week (about $1.50) at first, and seven shillings afterwards, and with such an income he could afford only a penny loaf and a pennyworth of milk for breakfast, with another loaf and a bit of cheese for supper. Dinner, a slice of pudding or a sausage, perhaps, he bought at some place near the warehouse, and so his days were passed without companions, without schooling, without books, without amusements, lonely and alone. Yet he washed away at his bottles with all the skill he could muster, and told his troubles to no one, presenting so old and worldly-wise an appearance that the helpless Micawbers confided in and leaned upon him.

Mr. Micawber's difficulties coming to a head, so to speak, he was sent to Debtors' Prison; but David took a tiny room near by, that he might not quite lose his only friends. It was clear, however, that when the Micawber difficulties were finally settled, the family must leave London and make a fresh start elsewhere, and David meditated day and night upon a certain resolution that he had taken. He confided it to no one, but wrote to his old nurse, Peggotty, asking her to lend him half a guinea for a special purpose, and inquiring, casually, if she remembered where the great-aunt lived who had called at Blunderstone Rookery the day he was born.

Receiving the money and the answer, he saw the Micawber family off on the stage-coach, completed his week's work at the warehouse, packed and labeled his box, and set off for Dover to confide himself and his now unbearable trials to Miss Betsey Trotwood.

At that time of his life, David seemed to attract troubles as a magnet does iron-filings; so you will not be surprised to learn that before he even reached the Dover coach-office his box and his money were stolen from him by a vicious and long-legged young man with a donkey-cart.

But David's resolution remained unaltered, and indeed the life that lay behind him was so hard and so cruel that he must needs press forward to a new one, whatever it might be. With three half-pence in his pocket, he set out upon the road to Dover, and, pawning his waistcoat here, and his jacket there, to get money for food, sleeping under haystacks, resting under friendly trees, now and then, when he was too footsore to go on, he tramped the dusty ways for six long days to seek the only person left of all his kith and kin.

But such courage and such perseverance never go unrewarded, and at last the boy, sunburned, tousle-headed, dirty, ragged, almost exhausted, found his way, by much inquiry, to the very house, surrounded with blooming flowers, where lived Miss Betsey Trotwood.

So surprised was that lady when the small and dusty tramp timidly touched her with his finger as she knelt, weeding in the garden, and said, "If you please, aunt, I am your nephew," that she sat flat down in the path and stared at him. When he had told her his story, however, as well as he could in his fright and fatigue, and burst at the end into a passion of crying, she carried him at once to the parlor, laid him on the sofa, and sent immediately for "Mr. Dick," a harmless, crack-brained old gentleman whom she had befriended and cared for. Nobody but Aunt Betsey ever sought advice of Mr. Dick; but when the circumstances had been explained to him and he was asked what should be done with her nephew, he replied, very sensibly and readily, "Wash him!" and, afterwards, "Give him his supper and put him to bed!" It was good advice and readily taken by David's aunt, and when in a few days the boy was rested and refreshed, and could tell his pitiful story more fully and clearly, Miss Betsey went wholly and unconditionally over to his side and promised that he should be her charge and that she never would give him up or desert him.

So the troubled stream of David's life, vexed as it had been with many a painful obstacle, broadened out at last into placid waters flowing between grassy banks and fringed by willows.

A fine new school was found for him in the neighboring cathedral town of Canterbury, a pleasant lodging was secured during school-days with his aunt's lawyer, Mr. Wickfield, and with dear Agnes, his little daughter and house-keeper, and a real home was his every week-end, with the love and protection and companionship of Aunt Betsey and Mr. Dick.

Of David's progress as a youth and as a man, of his old friends, Traddles, Steerforth, and the Micawbers, of his enemy, the red-haired, bony, malignant Uriah Heap, of the faithful Peggotty, of Little Em'ly, of the charming Dora and her dog, Tip—of all these you shall learn more in that golden book of Charles Dickens which he called *The Personal History and Experience of David Copperfield, the Younger.*

# ℒITTℒℰ WOℳℰℕ

HEN we speak of a girl as "a little woman," we mean, I suppose, that she is, in miniature, what a grown woman is, or ought to be; that she is the bud of what the poet calls "A perfect woman, nobly planned, To warn, to comfort, and command," and, in their varying ways and in their varying degrees, just this were Meg and Jo, Beth and Amy March.

"Little Women," by Louisa M. Alcott, the book that tells us of their characters, their home life, their joys and their sorrows, has become one of the most famous stories for girls in all the world. Every public library has several copies on its shelves, in many homes it is a treasured possession, and every girl-foreigner who comes to these shores, be she Lithuanian, Armenian, Czecho-Slovak, or anything else, hugs it to her breast as soon as she can read English.

> Little Indian, Sioux or Crow,
> Little frosty Eskimo—

these read it in their wigwams and their igloos, or, if they have no bookstores handy and cannot get it, at least they wish they could.

Why is this book so beloved, you wonder? Why is it read and re-read and read over again till its pages are stained and tattered and its binding falls off from overmuch handling? Is it because its heroines are rich and beautiful? Not at all; they are just nice girls, living in an ordinary home on a very small income. Is it because they have thrilling adventures? Not in the least; nothing happens to them that might not happen to any girl you know. Is it that they attain great heights of distinction and win fame and fortune? Not a bit of it; only one of them has any idea of a career, and she does not "career" very long.

Why is it, then? Listen and let me try to explain its charm and its success.

You can distinguish the four March girls in the picture—Meg, demure and romantic; Jo, spirited and original; Beth, gentle and musical; Amy, artistic and esthetic; and this blooming nosegay of maidens is held together with a silver ribbon on which is lettered plainly: Love—Duty—Obedience!

Meg is like a rose; Jo, a spicy-sweet carnation; Beth, a sprig of mignonette; and Amy, a lily, gold and white and decorative. But the rose was not without a thorn, nor the other flowers flawless; Meg was inclined to be a little envious of the good fortune of other girls, and a little discontented with her lot; Jo was impatient and quick-tempered; Amy, a bit priggish and affected; and Beth—no, Beth had no faults—she was just a child-angel sent on earth for a while to help and comfort erring mortals.

As to the other three, if they had been perfection they would not have been real girls, and you could not have wept over their trials and laughed over their pleasures.

If the proper study of mankind is man, and we have the authority of a great poet for the saying, then the proper study of girlkind must be girls; and it is a branch of education to which boys, too, are not averse. So, although in the beginning of the story, at least, there is but one hero to four heroines, we shall find as we progress that other heroes mysteriously appear, as they are likely to do when princesses are sufficiently attractive.

The story of "Little Women" is set in the time of the Civil War, more than a century ago now; and Mr. March, father of the family, minister of a small parish somewhere in New England, had gone to the front with the troops as a chaplain, when the book opens. Mrs. March, the beloved "Marmee" of the story, was busily working with the Soldiers' Aid Society, and Meg and Jo, the two older girls, were both at work also, helping along the family fortunes. Meg was visiting governess in a family of rather spoiled and disagreeable children, and Jo went daily to her Aunt March to read aloud, run errands, and do anything else which that severe and fault-finding old lady might desire.

Beth's peculiar trial amid these hard times was that music lessons could not be afforded for her, and that but little melody could be coaxed from the jangling keys of her old piano; while Amy fretted at having to wear her cousin's made-over dresses, and especially and always bewailed the unfortunate shape of her rather flat nose!

Next door to the March family lived an old gentleman of large fortune, and with him his grandson, Theodore Lawrence, always called Laurie in the book. Laurie had everything that heart could wish, so the girls thought— a luxurious house with fine furnishings and a fine piano, horses and carriages, money, books, no work to do unless he chose, and no one to interfere with his plans and pleasures.

Laurie, on the other hand, thought the family in the little brown house had everything that the world could give and that he most desired— father, mother, love, and companionship; and as he watched the laughing, rosy girls from his window, heard them singing with their mother, or through an uncurtained window saw them clustered around the lamp at night, he would have given all his luxuries for some of their happiness.

At a New Year's dance to which the two elder girls were invited, they first met Laurie, though they had almost decided that they would not go at all because of pronounced defects in their toilettes. They had to wear their "everlasting poplins," though they longed for silks; and they had only one pair of good gloves between them, careless Jo having ruined hers at their last party. She had burned her dress, too, in the back breadths, and had had to set in a piece; but that could be remedied by declining to dance and standing with her back to the wall, while, as she suggested, each sister could wear one good glove and carry a soiled one carelessly in her hand. She unfortunately insisted, when they were nearly ready, upon pinching Meg's curls around the face with a hot iron to hasten the drying process, the experiment resulting in tears on both sides and a row of little scorched bundles laid on the bureau before the victim.

Such was Jo—haphazard, careless, boyish, helter-skelter, everybody's favorite in the book, I think, and certainly the author's favorite, for she draws her with tenfold the skill that she bestows upon her sisters.

Feeling "as much out of place as a colt in a flower garden," Jo stood for-lornly at the party with her back to the wall, and finally slipped into a cur-tained recess where she found "that Lawrence boy," as shy and as uncom-fortable as she. So began the long and warm friendship that runs through the book until its end, for the two interested, amused, and delighted each other from the very first, and through Jo, Laurie became almost a member of the March family and shared in its joys and sorrows.

One of the pleasures of the March girls was private theatricals, very private and no gentlemen admitted, so that Laurie only heard of these fes-tivities at second hand. Jo, who had a decided literary turn, always wrote the plays and managed them, serving, too, as hero and villain alternately, being provided with a pair of long russet boots which "a lady who knew an actor" had lent her. Meg swept the stage in white robes as heroine, her long hair floating about her and her tuneful voice raised in song, or appeared as a witch with gray elf-locks hanging about her face, while the younger girls filled in minor parts as they were able.

There was a splendid performance on one occasion of "The Witches' Curse: an Operatic Tragedy," wherein the lovely heroine, imprisoned in a carefully constructed tower, prepared to fly with her lover, waiting (in the russet boots) below; but, catching her train as she descended, fell upon him, tower and all, and all three tumbled into the footlights. This unexpected close to the scene so convulsed the audience, seated upon a cot-bed in the back parlor, and so rocked them with merriment, that they, too, collapsed with the bed and were pulled out, heels first, with great difficulty.

"The Pickwick Club," which held its meetings in the garret, and which published a weekly paper called "The Pickwick Portfolio," was another family institution. At seven o'clock on Saturday evenings the four members ascended to the club-room, tied their badges around their heads, and took their seats. They all adopted names from Charles Dickens's "Pickwick Papers," Meg, as the eldest, being Mr. Pickwick himself; Jo, being of a literary turn, Augustus Snodgrass; Beth, because she was round and rosy, Tracy Tupman; and Amy, who was always trying to do what she couldn't, Nathaniel Winkle. Everybody contributed to the "Portfolio," and the President read aloud all contributions, prose and verse. Jo so managed as to have Laurie made a member of the sacred circle, and he, taking the name of the immortal Samuel Weller, immediately presented the Society with a post-office, conveniently located in the hedge between the two houses. "It's the old martin-house," explained Laurie, "and letters, manuscripts, books, and bundles can be placed in there. Allow me to present the Club Key; and with many thanks for your favor, take my seat."

That post-office, in coming days, held many a precious note and many a tender secret and proved a great convenience for the new member himself, but of that nobody yet dreamed on those frolicsome Saturday nights.

Life is not all "beer and skittles," however, as the original Samuel Weller would have said, and the girls had many small trials in their early years, and by and by some larger ones.

Amy, one day, took some pickled limes to school—delicious fruit, but strictly forbidden there—and, her crime being discovered, she was not only feruled smartly but made to stand on the platform alone for fifteen minutes; Meg went away to make a visit with some girl friends, and found to her sorrow that fine feathers do not make fine birds; Jo quarreled with Amy, who, as quick-tempered as her sister, in revenge burned up that sister's precious book which she was laboriously copying out in the garret.

Marmee saw and heard all these things, and sorrowed that her birds could not always agree in their little nest, but she also saw that for every wrong done there was sincere repentance, and that the bond of love between the sisters, though strained now and then, never gave way entirely.

When the girls were little, they had delighted to play "Pilgrim's Progress," to have their mother tie her piece-bags on their backs for burdens, give them hats and sticks and rolls of paper, and let them travel through the house from the cellar, which was the City of Destruction, up, up, to the housetop, where they had all the lovely things they could collect to make a Celestial City.

So the little pilgrims were climbing now in spirit, rising a step or two each day, and so they still did in body, sometimes, for Laurie, looking out from his window one autumn afternoon, saw them equipped with flapping hats and long staves, walking quietly through the garden and climbing the hill back of the house. When he crept after them and begged to join in whatever they were doing, Meg graciously explained the object of their journey, telling him that they called the hill the "Delectable Mountain," for "through an opening in the wood they could look into the sunset sky where, rising high into the ruddy light, were silvery white peaks that shone like the spires of some Celestial City."

It was not long after this day that Mr. March, still at the front, was stricken with serious illness, and Marmee was telegraphed for to nurse him. Laurie's tutor, John Brooke, a young man whom we have not yet met, but who had long been gazing ardently across the hedge at Meg's growing love-liness, was offered by old Mr. Lawrence to escort Marmee to Washington, and the four girls were left to keep house as best they might, under the guidance of Hannah, their faithful friend, companion, and maid-of-all-work.

All the loving daughters helped to further their mother's preparations; but it was left for Jo, generous and impetuous as usual, to sell her beautiful hair "to make father comfortable and bring him home sooner," and every girl who reads the scene feels a choke and a catch in her throat as Jo lays the precious roll of bills upon the table.

Following the well-known rule that misfortunes never come singly, Beth was laid low with scarlet fever as soon as her mother had gone, Jo, her favorite sister, installed as head nurse, and Amy packed off to Aunt March's, out of the reach of infection. Beth recovered partially and for a time, and father returned, well and strong again, to take his place with mother by the Christmas fire.

But things had begun to change now, and the little women to grow swiftly from buds to fully opened flowers. Meg and John Brooke were soon declared lovers, and Laurie was constantly devoted and attentive to his com-rade, Jo; but she, "thorny" as ever, declined to think of him in any other than a friendly light. It is true that her chief interest now was literature, for she had begun to be successful as a writer, and her stories and poems not only gave joy to her public, but the substantial rewards they earned made the life of the household an easier one. Wedded to her work, she thought the less of Laurie; but Miss Alcott's pen made that young hero of hers so attractive that almost every girl who meets him in the book would like to annex him for her own, and, failing that, cannot console herself that Jo was not so minded.

By and by, when Meg was Mrs. John Brooke, with her twins, Daisy and Demi, in her arms; when blessed Beth—"Little Tranquillity" as her father called her—had flown back to the heaven that claimed her; then Laurie turned to Amy, who had always looked up to and adored him in secret. It is well perhaps, but not quite what we had hoped, for Jo is our delight and our favorite, and we are not sure that we altogether approve of Friedrich Baer, the German professor, with whom our headlong heroine finally tumbled into love. It is true that he was manly, strong, and gentle, and greatly loved his "Heart's Dearest," as he called her; so we may leave her safely in his care, as indeed we must, for she herself decided it and gloried in her choice.

"And so, after many troubles, the Pilgrims came to a pleasant green meadow where lilies bloomed all the year round, and there they rested happily before they went on to their journey's end. And as they tarried in that place, they heard the Shepherd-boy singing:

> "Fullness to them a burden is,
>    That go on pilgrimage;
> Here little, and hereafter bliss,
>    Is best from age to age."

# JACKANAPES

RS. EWING—Juliana Horatia Ewing—who has given us this exquisite little story of Jackanapes and his brief career, knew well the subject and the background she was treating, for, like her hero, she was born in a quaint, old-fashioned English village, and as an English officer's wife she was familiar with "battle's magnificently stern array."

No doubt you know other books by Mrs. Ewing—"Six to Sixteen," perhaps, "Lob-lie-by-the-Fire," or "The Story of a Short Life," which is warranted to bring tears to the eyes of any reader, be he young or old. There is much that is tear-bringing in Jackanapes too, but the tears are of the kind that fall softly upon buds of love and kindly deeds and bring them to full blossom.

If I were transforming Jackanapes into a motion picture, and I believe it would make a very good one, I should set down the characters as follows, "in the order of their appearance," as the playbills say.

## CAST OF CHARACTERS

The Gray Goose
Big Miss Jessamine
Little Miss Jessamine (afterward Mrs. Black Captain)
The Black Captain
The Postman
The Doctor
Jackanapes

Master Tony Johnson
The Gardener's Son (afterward the Trumpeter)
The Gypsy Lad
Lollo, the red-haired Pony
The Gypsy Father
The General


And now let the music play and the curtain rise, for the performance is about to begin.  Better let the music be something martial, like "See, the Conquering Hero Comes," for the trumpet calls and the drums beat all through the tale.

It was an old, old English village where Jackanapes was born, and the time of the story is before and after the Battle of Waterloo, and everybody who ever went to school knows when that was; but, if anybody does not, he would find it to his advantage to look it up in the encyclopedia.

Those were the days when all England was apprehensive about a possible invasion of the country by the famous general, Napoleon Bonaparte, and his troops, and when unprincipled nurses frightened their small charges into fits by threatening that "Boney would get them" if they were not good. Outside of this perpetual fear—and it was a natural one, for the Channel was narrow and France very near—the village days were quiet ones.  No railway and no telegraph wires yet connected the village with London, and the news of the great War and the famous battles, Trafalgar, Salamanca, Vittoria, Waterloo, came down by mail-coach.  The coach was always dressed with flowers and oak leaves when it brought the news of victory, and the guard wore a laurel wreath above his royal livery.  All the village gathered at the "George and Dragon" on these days to hear the news, and the Gray Goose left the Green and sought a quieter place, far from the haunts of men.

On days when no mail-coach was to be expected, never was there a quieter place.  The old, black-timbered, whitewashed cottages sat sociably about the Green, each one with its fragrant garden of sweet peas and honeysuckle and poppies and roses; the donkeys grazed there, unmolested; the geese hissed and waddled about the pond in the center; and at night the men and boys played cricket on the soft turf, deep and green with ages of tending.

The Gray Goose really opens the story, for she saw all of it, was there when it began, and was living there when it ended, though it is not to be supposed that she thoroughly understood all that passed before her wise old eyes.  Yes, she was old, though the exact number of her years she could not compute; it seemed to confuse her head, somehow.  She counted time by the coming and going of Michaelmas; last Michaelmas such a thing happened; next Michaelmas it may be supposed to happen again; etc., etc.  There may have been unfortunate events in her family which imprinted this date upon her mind, for roast goose on Michaelmas Day is a favorite dish in England.

However this may be, the Gray Goose knew all the people in the story.  She was well acquainted with Big Miss Jessamine, who lived in one of the prettiest black and white houses on the Green; and she greatly admired Little Miss Jessamine and her wonderful ripples of golden hair, shining on Sundays, when it had just been washed, like the moon in the pond on a clear night.  The Goose always claimed, too, that she had been the first to see the Black Captain, and that she had never been afraid of him—not she, she was no such goose as that!

It was not at all understood in the village, at first, why the Black Captain was there at all, nor why he was constantly dashing about the lanes on his coal-black mare.  There was some disposition on the part of the nurses to have him "fetch naughty children away," like that ogre, Napoleon Bonaparte; but by and by he was regarded with a kindlier eye, for everybody could see

*David Copperfield*

PAGE 1

*Little Women*

PAGE 10

Tiny Tim and Bob Cratchit, in *A Christmas Carol*

*Hans Brinker*

PAGE 36

that he was dancing attendance upon Little Miss Jessamine, whom everybody loved.

It was learned that Big Miss Jessamine did not look with favor upon the Black Captain's advances, for she thought her lovely niece too young to marry anybody, much less a dashing soldier on a dancing, prancing, satin-skinned mare. When the villagers heard that the old General, the Captain's father, was equally against the match, on the ground that their young lady was not good enough for his son, they were aghast at the idea, and the Gray Goose was known to have hissed violently when the Captain passed the pond. It was not long, however, before a clattering of horse's hoofs was heard through the village in the middle of the night, and in the morning everybody knew that the Black Captain had carried Little Miss Jessamine away behind him on his coal-black mare, and married her at Gretna Green, though why, as the Gray Goose said, their own Green wasn't good enough for a wedding, she was sure *she* didn't know!

The villagers said that the reckless young couple would never again be seen in the village; but they were mistaken, for in less than a week they were back again, forgiven by Big Miss Jessamine, and they were the happiest of the happy, wandering along the lanes together, gathering blackberries for jam, and making bryony wreaths for each other. The Postman, who was an old soldier, delighted to meet them on his route and to give the Captain the proper salute, to show that he had not forgotten how to respect an officer.

But those were trying times! One afternoon the black mare was stepping gently up and down the grass, with her head at her master's shoulder and as many children crowded on her silky back as if she had been an elephant in a menagerie; and the next afternoon she carried her master away to his regiment, the old Postman waiting for him, rigid with salutation, at the four cross-roads.

Bad times, indeed, and all the horrors of war! Mrs. Black Captain, once Little Miss Jessamine, lived only for the arrival of the mail-coach and the news from the front; and though she was pining away with grief and anxiety, she managed to get to the "George and Dragon" almost every day. Yet at the last she was not strong enough to go, and when the Postman brought the newspaper with the news of the glorious victory of Waterloo, her old aunt was forced to read to her the list of the dead, which began with a royal Duke, and ended, alas, with the Black Captain!

Not all those who are wounded by war, you know, are to be found in the printed list of casualties, and though it was not three days before the young wife had joined her husband, her name is not to be found among those killed at Waterloo. Big Miss Jessamine, bowed with grief, knelt by the cradle of their orphan son, a tiny morsel with a sheen of golden hair already on his head, and anxiously asked of the Doctor: "Will he live? *Can* he live?"

"Live, madam?" cried the Doctor; "just look at him! He's as strong as a lion, the young Jackanapes!"

So Jackanapes he was called, although at the proper time he was christened Theodore; and Jackanapes he grew up, and so was known not only by the Gray Goose and the village at large, but by his especial cronies, Master Tony Johnson and Master Tony Johnson's father's gardener's youngest son.

The three companions, first toddling babies, then restless, active little lads, played about the Green, went to the village fairs, rode the wooden horses in the merry-go-rounds, and had the best of all possible times every day in the year. Big Miss Jessamine had had no experience in bringing up boys; but this one, with his golden mop of hair, she loved so dearly that her love brought her wisdom, and Jackanapes grew up obedient, honorable, and kind-hearted.

He was devoted to horses, rode the donkeys on the Green whenever they would let him, and stuck to "Black Prince" in the merry-go-round when poor Tony Johnson fell off his mount, pale of face and sick at heart. After fair-time, one year, Jackanapes met a gypsy lad on the Green, with a fascinating red-haired pony; and, managing to get a ride on the pony's back, he delighted in his speed, the clatter of his hoofs, and the blowing of his mane in the wind. He thought of Lollo, as the gypsy lad called him, by day and dreamed of him by night, and at last made his way out of the village to a Common where the tribe was camped, to inquire the price of the treasure.

The gypsy father, smoking a dirty pipe the while, agreed that Lollo was a nice pony and a racer, and that he might be bought for "fifteen pound" (about $75); but as fifteen hundred pounds would have been as easy to get, Jackanapes turned away, very sorrowful.

By the time these things were happening, the war was over, Napoleon had been banished to St. Helena, and the General, home from France, wrote that he was coming to the village to see his grandson for the first time. Great excitement and nervousness on the part of Big Miss Jessamine; great excitement and no nervousness at all on the part of Jackanapes; but he listened to all his aunt said, and promised to obey. He was to try to keep his clothes and his hands clean, and his mop of yellow hair smooth; not to burst in at the parlor door; not to talk at the top of his voice; to be sure to say "sir" to the General; and to rub his shoes on the doormat.

The General came, and proved to be a delightful person with just ideas as to the tastes and ways of boys. When Jackanapes told him about Lollo, he was immensely interested, and thought it very likely that he might buy him for himself. Jackanapes was of the opinion that the General might be too tall for Lollo; but the old officer remarked that, if so, he "could double up his legs"; and the gypsy and the pony were sent for at once. The General well remembered the day when he had first set his son, the Black Captain, on a horse, and he thought of it again with moistened eyes as the gypsy lifted Jackanapes to Lollo's back and suggested that he show his grandfather the pony's paces.

Taking from his pocket a little trumpet that he had bought at the last fair, Jackanapes blew a shrill blast and was off like the wind, his hair flying, and the Gray Goose squawking wildly as she fled across the Green. Gypsy and grandfather applauded the performance, and Lollo was bought at once and presented to the young rider, who was as astonished by the gift as he was delighted. That very night he confided to the General that, though Big Miss Jessamine could not bear to hear of it, he had made up his mind to be a soldier like his father and his grandfather, and that nothing, either now or ever, could possibly change his mind. The General heard, looking down into the eager eyes so like those that had closed at Waterloo, and promised that it should be so, and that when the time came Jackanapes should have a commission in the cavalry.

"If you live to be an honor to your country," said his grandfather, "this old heart shall grow young again with pride for you; and if you die in the service of your country—God bless me, it can but break for you!"

.    .    .    .    .    .    .    .    .    .

It was twenty years after this when the story ended. The General was dead, the friendly Postman had gone, too, and Big Miss Jessamine, though still active and keen in mind, was an old lady, taking her airings in a Bath-chair drawn by Lollo, the red-haired pony of long ago.

The Gray Goose was still alive and in good feather, and Jackanapes was a cavalry officer now, as he had longed to be. Another war was raging, and he was at the front with his regiment. There, too, was Master Tony Johnson, and doing his very best, although his ability as a horseman was not much greater than it had been in the days of the merry-go-rounds. There, too, was Tony's father's gardener's youngest son, a Trumpeter now—a very young one, but grave with the might of care and responsibility.

"Sound Retire!" he had been bidden in the midst of the battle, and he had done as he was bid, though what between the smoke and the dust and the hard-mouthed horse he was riding, he hardly knew why or where the troops were falling back, or if they were likely to lose the fight.

He did see, and see with pride, Jackanapes whirling about on his wonderful horse, the red charger named for Lollo, that had borne him in every battle, and he saw the golden hair gleam in the sunshine, for a blow had bared it. Where now was Jackanapes galloping, his head laid close to Lollo's ear! What was happening there in the noise and smoke?

Alas! poor Tony Johnson, unlucky as ever, had been thrown from his wretched mount at the very moment when it was life or death to ride away, and the struggling beast had crushed his master's leg as he tried to rise. Jackanapes had seen it all—when did he ever fail to see a friend in trouble? —and he was rushing to the rescue.

In spite of all Tony's prayers that he would leave him, Jackanapes caught him up in a moment, flung him across his saddle, told him to keep his head down, and galloped away with him after the retreating troops.

There came a moment when the enemy seemed to spring up in all directions, and Tony, seeing that his side was losing ground, cried out in agony, "Jackanapes, Jackanapes, if you love me, leave me!"

"Leave you?" cried Jackanapes, shaking his mop of hair. "To save my skin? No, Tony, not to save my soul!"

Perhaps it was the light on the golden head that made it so good a target. Be that as it may, it fell at the next shot; and it was Tony, clumsy, unlucky Tony, who was saved.

Poor Jackanapes, you say; a life wasted that might have been so useful to the world!

Yes, but *was* it wasted?  Did the parson think so when he preached Jackanapes's funeral sermon on the text, "Whosoever will save his life shall lose it; and whosoever will lose his life for my sake shall find it?"  Did the village think so, as it wept to hear?

No—"Greater love hath no man than this, that a man lay down his life for his friend," and we may be sure that, like Mr. Valiant in "Pilgrim's Progress," when Jackanapes passed over, all the trumpets sounded for him on the other side.

# TINY TIM

A CHRISTMAS CAROL, by Charles Dickens, is one of the most famous of all the Christmas tales in the English language, and in many households it is read aloud by the fireside at every succeeding season, and people hear it through a mist of smiles and tears. It has the very breath and spirit of Christmas in it, and, as you read, the walls dress themselves with holly, mistletoe hangs in the doorway, church bells ring and sleigh bells tinkle out-of-doors, and on the frosty air come floating delicious odors of plum pudding, red-hot chestnuts, spicy mince pies, cherry-cheeked apples, luscious grapes, and slowly browning turkey.

The book has a very picture-gallery of people in it, and Timothy Cratchit, youngest child of Robert Cratchit, Esquire, is but one tiny figure among the many. He is like a miniature painted on ivory which does not hang upon the wall, but lies with others of its kind upon a velvet cushion in a glass case; and yet his is the face we love the best in the book, and the one that comes most clearly to us when the Christmas carols sound.

You can see him in the picture, standing by his father at the Christmas service—fair-haired, blue-eyed, with just a hint of rose in his cheeks, and his sweet lips a bit apart as he joins with the boy choir in:

> Hark, the herald angels sing,
> Glory to the new-born King!

His little crutch stands beside him in the pew, for he is also a little lame prince, like another boy in this picture book of yours, but far happier than that royal lad because he has a good and loving father and mother and a bevy of brothers and sisters.

If there is any hero in the book, I suppose it is Scrooge, Ebenezer Scrooge, the employer of Tim's father, though it is hard to make a hero out of a man whose very name sounds like a creaking door, or a dull saw trying to cut through a tough plank.  We have it on Dickens's own written word that Scrooge was a "squeezing, wrenching, grasping, scraping, clutching, covetous old sinner," and that he was "hard and sharp as flint, secret and self-contained, and solitary as an oyster!"

Pretty material for a hero, isn't it?  But by and by, when you read the book, you will see how the Three Spirits—the Ghosts of Christmas Past, of Present, and of Future—so worked upon the hard old heart, far down in the depths of hard old Scrooge, that it began to beat again, to send rich blood coursing through his veins, and to stimulate him to kind words and deeds.

Ebenezer Scrooge was Bob Cratchit's employer, as before said, and Bob was the father of tiny, crippled Tim, of Martha, of Belinda, of Peter, and also of two middle-sized Cratchits, like the middle-sized Bear—neither so big as the biggest, nor so small as the smallest.  That was a large family to keep, even had Mr. Cratchit's been an equally large salary; but, as it was, it is no wonder that poor Bob never could afford an overcoat, but wore instead a white comforter around his neck, closely wrapped, with the ends hanging down below his waist.

The book begins on Christmas Eve, in Mr. Scrooge's office, and he is crosser than the crossest Turk in Constantinople, wishing there were no such day as Christmas, fiercely refusing his nephew's invitation to dinner, grudging poor Bob his holiday at home, and declining to give one penny to some gentlemen who come to ask him for a subscription for the poor.

"If there are so many of the poor as you say," said Scrooge, sharply, "they'd better die and decrease the surplus population. I have enough to do to mind my own business. Good evening, gentlemen!"

Satisfied with having made everybody about him "as unhappy as the stones in the road," as they say in France, old Scrooge went home to his lonely house and his lonely room; and by and by, while he was still minding his own business, the Ghost of Christmas Past came to his bedside and constrained him to walk abroad with him.

Of course Scrooge was afraid; not because the Spirit wore a frightful form, for indeed his face was fair, and he bore a sprig of greenest holly in his hand. No, it was not that; but because the unearthly visitant proclaimed that he was the Ghost of Christmas Past, and would bear Scrooge through the window and abroad upon the air to visit again the scenes of his boyhood.

Only the day before he had growled in his office: "Out upon Merry Christmas! A fig for the Season! What's Christmas time to me?" and now he was to see what it had been to him in youth, and so refresh his withered heart with the dews of memory.

Scrooge and the Spirit soared above the little town where he was born, and saw the merry boys on their shaggy ponies, laughing and shouting, and calling Christmas greetings to one another as they parted at the cross-roads for their several homes. They saw the old boarding-school where Scrooge had been left once for the holidays, and the lonely boy sitting there without companions, save those in the books he was reading. They saw the long-dead little sister running to throw her arms about his neck and to tell him they were to spend Christmas together, and by and by when Scrooge had grown older, they saw the warehouse where he had been employed in London, and the wonderful Christmas party given by Mr. and Mrs. Fezziwig to everybody employed in the house and in the business.

It is of no use for me to try to tell you about that party—nobody but

Charles Dickens could have described it or could have told how they sang and talked and danced and feasted and were gaily and innocently happy. Scrooge felt it all—oh, yes, he remembered it—and when the Spirit looked on him intently, he saw a tear upon Scrooge's furrowed cheek.

When the first aërial journey was over, Scrooge sank to sleep again in his own bed, and never wakened till the bell in the neighboring church struck One! when, not much to his surprise, for nothing could surprise him now, he found that he lay in a blaze of ruddy light that streamed from the adjoining room. Creeping softly to the door and peeping in, he saw a jolly Giant, robed in green, a holly wreath upon his curls, bearing in his hand a glowing torch shaped like Plenty's horn.

"I am the Ghost of Christmas Present," cried the figure. "Hold fast to my robe and we will fare abroad and see how the world keeps holiday at this most blessed time of all the year."

Scrooge had learned many things of the Ghost of Christmas Past, and now he was submissive and ready to follow the new Spirit whithersoever he might go.

In a moment they stood in the winter streets, and saw the people shoveling away the snow and calling Merry Christmas to their neighbors; they saw the grocers' and fruiterers' windows, overflowing with dainties; they heard the bells ringing, and saw the families trooping to church, and then they soared on high, far over the land, and saw that in shepherds' huts upon the moors, deep down in mines, in lonely lighthouses, on ships at sea, even in prisons and among the convicts there was no man who had not a kinder word for another on that day and who had not remembered those he cared for with a warmer heart.

They went to many poor and humble houses, too, but to none among them all happier than Bob Cratchit's—Scrooge's ill-paid clerk. Bob and

Tiny Tim had gone to church, but everybody else was at home save Martha, the eldest girl, and everybody was either preparing dinner, expecting dinner, talking about dinner, or smelling dinner; and everybody was dressed for the occasion, including Peter, who proudly wore his father's collar.

Then in came Martha, who was a dressmaker's helper and had been detained by press of work; and then Bob himself with Tiny Tim upon his shoulder. Of course great rejoicing followed over the united family, and presently Tim was borne off by the two middle-sized Cratchits that he might hear the Christmas pudding singing as it boiled.

"And how did little Tim behave at church?" asked Mrs. Cratchit.

"As good as gold," said Bob, "and better. Somehow he gets thoughtful, sitting by himself so much, and thinks the strangest things you ever heard. He told me, coming home, that he hoped the people saw him in the church, because he was a cripple, and it might be pleasant for them to remember, upon Christmas Day, who made lame beggars walk and blind men see."

The father, and the mother, too, were a little tremulous and tearful as Tim's words were repeated, for indeed the little lad was far from strong, but in a moment the tap of his crutch was heard, and it was announced that dinner was ready!

There was a roast goose for dinner, but there was as much excitement about it as if it had been a hippogriff or a unicorn, and, indeed, one was about as rare as the other in that household. There were mashed potatoes, too, and apple sauce; and there was certainly plenty of these, even if the goose was not so very big. And then there was a pudding—a perfectly wonderful pudding—and everybody admired it and exclaimed about it and feasted on it, and nobody said or thought that it was at all a small pudding for such a large family. "Any Cratchit would have blushed to hint at such a thing!"

You can fancy how old Scrooge felt while he and the Spirit looked upon these things, and how he marveled at the happiness the Day had brought to these humble people. He noted Tiny Tim especially, sitting by his father's side when the dinner was over, and when good little Bob cried: "A Merry Christmas to us all, my dears; God bless us," he heard, with tears, how Tim echoed, "God bless us, every one!"

"The little lad seems very frail," said Scrooge to the Spirit, anxiously. "Tell me if he will live!"

"I see a vacant seat," replied the Ghost, "in the poor chimney-corner, and a crutch without an owner, carefully preserved. If these shadows remain unaltered by the Future, the child will die."

"No, no," said Scrooge. "Oh, no, kind Spirit! say he will be spared."

"What is his life to you?" returned the Ghost. "If he be like to die, he had better do it and decrease the 'surplus population.'"

Scrooge bent his head in penitence and grief to hear his own words thus quoted against him, and, as he did so, the Ghost of Christmas Present passed from sight.

Trembling with fear and with anxiety, the old man awaited in an open place the last of the Spirits—the Ghost of Christmas Yet-to-Come. He had learned much from the two former phantoms; his heart had begun to beat again, and he had begun to see more clearly what life might be in the future, not only to him but to those about him, but he dreaded, not without reason, that it was too late to change his fate, and that what he had willed in the past must now inevitably happen.

"Ghost of the Future!" Scrooge exclaimed, "I fear you more than any specter I have seen. But, as I know your purpose is to do me good, I am prepared to bear you company, and do it with a thankful heart. Will you not speak to me?"

The Spirit, shrouded in a deep black garment which concealed its face and form, made no reply but pointed onward, and Scrooge followed in the shadow of its dress, which seemed to bear him up.

They passed along the streets of London, and here and there heard men discussing the death of some old curmudgeon of a merchant for whom nobody seemed to care and to whose funeral nobody seemed willing to go. They looked into Scrooge's office, but a stranger sat in his accustomed corner. They saw in a dusty rag-shop a group of women who were selling some dead man's clothing and the furniture of his rooms; and all these things chilled Scrooge's blood and filled him with dread as to what he might see at his journey's end.

At last they entered poor Bob Cratchit's house and found the mother and children seated round the fire—but quiet, very quiet. The mother was sewing on some black material, but she laid her work upon the table suddenly and put her hand up to her face, saying the color hurt her eyes. "Is it not time for your father, children?" she asked.

"Past it, rather," Peter answered; "but I think he's walked a little slower than he used, these last few evenings, mother."

"I have known him to walk," said mother, "very fast—with Tim upon his shoulder—very fast indeed. But Tim was very light to carry, and his father loved him so that it was no trouble—never any trouble."

When Bob came in, Scrooge saw at once what had happened, and saw it with an aching heart. No Tiny Tim was there to meet Bob, and as soon as he had sat down the two middle-sized Cratchits got upon his knees and laid each child a little cheek against his face, as if they said, "Don't mind it, father; don't be grieved!"

The tears were so thick in Scrooge's eyes that he could hardly see, and his sobs shook him so that he followed the Spirit with difficulty as he sped away from that grief-stricken house, away, away to a lonely graveyard where, upon a neglected stone the carved letters EBENEZER SCROOGE were plainly to be seen.

Scrooge fell upon his knees before the Phantom at this sight, and begged that the name might be erased from the stone. "I am not the man I was!" he cried. "Assure me that I yet may change these shadows you have shown me by an altered life. I will honor Christmas in my heart, and try to keep it all the year. Have pity upon me, Spirit, that these things may not befall!"

He still knelt, holding up his hands in eager supplication, when he seemed to see an alteration in the Phantom's hood and dress. . . . It shrank, collapsed, and, wonder of wonders, it dwindled down to his own bed-post!

.    .    .    .    .    .    .    .    .    .    .

Yes, it really was his own bed-post. "The bed was his own, the room was his own, and, best and happiest of all, the time before him was his own, to make amends in. He scrambled out of bed, so happy that he could hardly stand. He rushed to the window, and there were the churches ringing out the lustiest peals he had ever heard: "Clash, clang, hammer, ding, dong, bell. Bell, dong, ding, hammer, clang, clash. Oh, glorious, glorious!"

"What day is this?" cried Scrooge to a boy in the street below.

"What!" returned the boy, with all his might of wonder. "Why, CHRISTMAS DAY!"

"Christmas Day!" thought Scrooge. "Then the Spirits must have done it all in one night. Why, it's wonderful! I can begin all over again!"

And he did begin all over again, and he did it immediately. He asked the boy in the street that very minute to go and buy the prize turkey at the corner and take it to the Cratchits'; he met in the square, when he went out, the very gentlemen who had asked him for help for the poor the previous day, and gave them such a sum that they nearly fainted where they stood; he went to his nephew's to dinner, and was the life of the party and next morning he was waiting in the counting-house when Bob Cratchit came, and raised his salary before the astonished fellow could wink.

Oh, no, indeed, Tiny Tim did not die; and by and by Scrooge was a second father to him and a help to all the family.

In fact, "Scrooge became as good a friend, as good a master, and as good a man as the good old city of London ever knew." It was always said of him, thereafter, that he knew how to keep Christmas well, if any man alive possessed the knowledge.

"May that be truly said of us, and all of us! And so, as Tiny Tim observed, God Bless Us, Every One!"

# *HANS BRINKER*

HAT do you think of when you hear the word Holland? Does a picture come before your eyes of windmills slowly turning against a watery-gray sky, of canals full-flowing between grassy banks, of many-colored tulips shining in the sun, of storks on red-tiled housetops, wooden shoes, snow-white caps, glittering window panes and a strange mingling of trees and masts wherever you look?

All these things indeed mean Holland; and when you are older and wiser the name will also mean to you long traditions of splendid fighting against oppression, of hardly gained religious liberty, of noble men and godly women. All these things, too, Mary Mapes Dodge greatly desired to make us see and feel in her book, "Hans Brinker, or The Silver Skates," which has long been a favorite among young people all over the world.

Hans and Gretel are the hero and heroine of the book, and they are well-known names to us all, for there are Hänsel and Gretel of Grimm's fairy tales—of course you know them—and the same brother and sister in the fairy opera, where the fearsome old witch throws a spell on wandering children and imprisons them in her sugar castle.

Hans Brinker and his sister, Gretel, however, are not at all fairy-like, but just sturdy Dutch children, Hans, about fifteen years old, with great square shoulders and bushy yellow hair, and Gretel, three years younger, with "a color on her cheeks like pink and white tulips when the wind is blowing."

Butler, an old English poet, speaks of Holland as

> A land that rides at anchor, and is moor'd,
> In which they do not live, but go aboard,

but the description does not fit the season in which this story opens, for it is midwinter, the canals are frozen deep, and Hans and Gretel, on their clumsy, home-made wooden skates, are gliding over the ice, chasing each other about, or making wonderful loops, shining spirals, and cat's cradles on the glassy surface.

It is, no doubt, delightful to live in a land where you can make one leap from your doorway to the ice, without any tiresome walking to the nearest pond or lake; but you must remember that it is not always winter, and that there must be many months when a full-fed stream flows by that same door. I understand that all babies' heads are fitted in Holland with pads stiffened with whalebone to protect their skulls should they fall: but I should think fins and tails would be more useful, for wherever they stumble it must be into water.

Geography lessons have already taught you that Holland is a level country with a vast network of waterways spreading all over it and protected from inundations from the restless, grasping ocean by great dikes, some of them so high and so broad that houses and even churches have been built upon them.

"And thereby hangs a tale," as Shakespeare said; in fact, two tales, for one is of the child-hero of Haarlem, who stopped the leak in the dike with his little hand, and stayed there on duty all night long till he was rescued, half-conscious, at daybreak.

The other tale concerns Hans and Gretel Brinker, and explains why they were forced to use wooden skates, why their clothing was shabby and patched, and why their mother, Dame Brinker, scraped and saved and spun and wove and knitted from morning until night. Ten years before the beginning of this story, Raff Brinker, a sober, industrious workman, fell from a scaffolding where a weak spot in a dike was being repaired, and was taken home insensible. "From that hour he never worked again; though he lived on, mind and memory were gone."

Gretel could not remember him save as a strange, silent man whose eyes followed her vacantly whichever way she turned; but Hans had recollections of a strong, cheerful father who was never tired of bearing him upon his shoulder.

Up to the time of this terrible fall, Raff and Meitje Brinker had been able to save money—sometimes even a guilder (about forty cents) every week—and the good wife had stored it away in an old stocking; but when, after her husband's accident, she went to look for the hoard which had now grown to a thousand guilders, behold, it was nowhere to be found! Not only could it not be found, but Raff could never afterwards understand nor answer her questions as to its whereabouts, and she vexed herself unceasingly as to what could have become of so much money, and why her man had taken it from its wonted hiding-place.

There was a certain scapegrace friend of her husband whom she had long suspected of a thievish hand, and her suspicions had been justified when five years ago he had gone to prison for robbery. Could he have stolen the guilders, she wondered, and when and how could he have found the opportunity?

"When your father came in to supper on the night he was hurt," she often told Hans, "he was just opening his lips to tell me something, when Broom Klatterboost came flying in with word that the dike was in danger. Your father, alack! caught up his tools and ran out, and that was the last I ever saw of him in his right mind. We shall never know any more of that good thousand guilders, children!" And here the troubled dame wiped away a tear.

"Nay, mother, do not cry!" whispered Hans, soothingly. "The father might wake some day and tell us all about it. I am strong, and growing older every year, and soon Gretel and I can earn enough to take care of us all."

They were good children, if Dame Brinker did say it herself, and both of them went out day after day at certain seasons of the year to cut and gather peat for fuel; while Hans was very clever at carving in wood, and often rode the towing-horses on the canal for a few stivers a day. Both, too, were fine gardeners, and Gretel tended geese for the neighboring farmers whenever she could.

Gretel could sing, and sew, and run on stilts, better than any girl for miles around, but she was not fond of books, while Hans held the post of honor in almost every class, and the boys who laughed at him out-of-doors, for his patched clothes and scant leather breeches, looked at him with respect in the schoolroom.

The brother and sister could go to school, however, only in the winter, and for the past month had been kept at home by their father's increasing illness and the growing need of earning money for the little household.

You, who are not yet required either to save or to earn, would have been sorry for Hans and Gretel as they glanced up now and then from their work on that fine winter's morning and saw the light-hearted, happy boys and girls flitting about on the canal. They knew them all by sight and name. There was Hilda van Gleck, the burgomaster's daughter, in furs and velvet; there was Annie Bouman (whose bright eyes Hans particularly admired) in her scarlet jacket and blue skirt; there was laughing Katrinka; and, flocking about the three, the lads—Carl Schummel, Peter and Ludwig van Holp, Jacob Poot, and a very small boy with the very large name of Voostenwalbert Schimmelpenninck.

Not only were young people skating for play, but many older ones were skimming to their work over the glittering ice. There were market-women with loads upon their heads, peddlers bending beneath packs, stately doctors and lawyers, and now and then a fat burgomaster on wonderful skates with superb strappings and dazzling runners, curving over the instep and topped with gilt balls.

Soon the boys and girls gathered together and began to talk about the skating race that was to be run on the birthday of Hilda van Gleck's mother and for which Hilda was to give prizes—silver skates for the girl, with bells on them. . . .

"You don't know anything about it!" cried Voostenwalbert Schimmel-penninck. "They haven't a sign of a bell on them!"

"Well, I hope Hilda knows," laughed Katrinka, as she skated around her in a graceful circle, "for she is going to give the prizes."

"The girl's pair *is* to have bells," pronounced Hilda, quietly; "and the boy's has an arrow engraved on the sides."

"Oh, what fun! We will all try for the prize!" cried the young people, and, chatting excitedly, they skimmed away to school like a flight of swallows.

At noontime, when all rushed out to skate again, Hans and Gretel came, too, to watch the sport. Carl Schummel jeered at the pair and their clumsy skates, and called them "little rag-pickers," but Hilda was of another make, and drew near to tell them about the skating-race and to ask them to compete with the others.

"Ah, young lady," answered Hans, respectfully, "even if we could enter, we could skate only a few strokes with the rest. Our skates are hard wood, you see; but they soon become damp, and then they stick and trip us."

Hilda wished then that she had a little more left of her month's allowance; but she asked the pair which of them was the better skater, and, on Hans saying it was Gretel, put eight kwartjes (about eighty cents) into his hand and told him to buy his sister a pair of skates for the race. She was gliding away when Hans ran after her, calling:

"Thank you, young lady, but we cannot take this money."

"Why not, indeed?" asked Hilda, flushing.

"Because we have not earned it," Hans replied, flushing in his turn.

Hilda was quick-witted, and she had noticed a pretty wooden chain about Gretel's neck. "Carve me a chain, then, Hans, like the one your sister wears."

"That I will, lady, with all my heart. We have whitewood in the house, fine as ivory. You shall have one tomorrow."

"Keep the money, then, and buy the skates," answered Hilda, and she slipped away.

Dame Brinker agreeing that Hilda's bargain was quite fair, Hans made and delivered the necklace and bought Gretel the long-desired skates, though indeed she begged that he would buy them for himself, instead. To this he would not hear, however, and watched with happy pride his little sister flying in and out among the skaters.

"By den donder!" exclaimed Peter van Holp to Carl Schummel, "but that little one in the patched petticoat skates well. She has toes on her heels and eyes in the back of her head! It will be a joke if she gets in the race and beats them all!"

Gretel's mother was sure, of course, that her nursling would "beat them all" if she tried; and she was exultant when Hans carved and sold another necklace and bought a pair of skates for himself. It was on this errand, as he scraped along on his wooden runners to Amsterdam, that he met on the ice the great Dr. Boekman, the most famous surgeon of Holland, whose likeness he had often seen in the shop windows.

Now Raff Brinker had grown much worse of late, violent at times, moaning constantly, and holding his head as if in pain. Hans had talked with his mother of asking Dr. Boekman to see the sufferer, but, knowing she had no money for his fee, the good dame would not consent. This, then, was the time, thought Hans, in spite of his mother's opposition, for there was the great doctor within arm's reach; and the lad, trembling with fear and excitement, ventured to shout to him and stop his flight. Dr. Boekman was none too willing to be stopped, for he was off to Leyden on a hurry call, but when he saw Hans's honest eyes, and heard his stammering voice explain that his father's ten years' illness had been caused by a fall from a dike, he agreed that he would come to see the poor man in a week's time, though he feared, and here he shook his head, that it was far too late to do anything now.

Cheered by the mere promise of a visit, Hans sped on to Amsterdam and secured the precious skates, though when he returned home even these were disregarded, for his father's condition had already changed for the worse. All was forgotten now but the danger that threatened the little household, and through Peter van Holp's kind offices, Hans was able to get a message to Dr. Boekman, urging him to come to them at once. Sure enough, the great man did come speedily, with his assistant and his wonderful instruments, and after a brief examination was able to say that a surgical operation might relieve the patient, if Dame Brinker were willing to take the risk of life or death involved.

White and tearful, the wife agreed that it should be done; for indeed there was no choice, since without the operation her man would be but a raving maniac before long. Her consent obtained, the trial was soon over, for the great surgeon proved magically skillful, his assistant deft and sure, and Hans won great praise from them both for his courage and his helpfulness.

When all was completed and, as Dr. Boekman believed, most successfully, Dame Brinker fell upon her knees at his feet in gratitude, and Hans, wringing the great man's hand, swore to pay whatever might be his fee though it took him half a lifetime to earn it. But the doctor laughed all this away and only cautioned the household to perfect quiet and to procure the best of nourishment for his patient.

"He must have the juice of fresh meat," said the doctor, "white bread, dried and toasted, and good Malaga wine," and, so saying, he took his leave.

"White bread, fresh meat, wine!" cried Dame Brinker, falling into her chair, despairingly. "As well say gold and jewels!" and she threw her apron over her head to sob behind it.

Hans comforted her again, promised that his father should have everything the doctor ordered, and vowed that if he could not find work to earn the money, he would sell the precious skates so that the night's meal at least should be provided. But this sacrifice was not required of him: indeed, it seemed as if the mere mention of skates worked like magic in the family, for before Raff Brinker had opened his eyes more than once and spoken a few intelligent words to his wondering wife, a great basket came from the good doctor with the dainties he had ordered, and a pair of soft, woolly blankets besides.

Now all was well in the little home. It was plain that Dr. Boekman's work had been successful, the father was himself again, in mind, at least, and they would only have to wait for his bodily strength to return.

"If we only had the thousand guilders now, mother," Hans said, softly, one evening, "we should have no more cause for anxiety, for that would care for father's every want till he is well again."

"I know," answered Dame Brinker, glancing toward the bed where the invalid lay sleeping; "but those thousand guilders will never be seen again in this world, my son!"

"A thousand guilders!" murmured a weak voice from the blankets. "Aye! I'm glad, wife, thou hast had them for thy needs these ten long years."

"Ask him, Hans," whispered his mother; "ask him quickly before he drops off again, what he did with the money."

The lad tiptoed to the bedside, made pretense of arranging the clothing, and, in as natural a voice as he could manage, asked: "What was it you did with the money, the night you were hurt, father? I forgot what you said."

"Willow-tree, willow-tree," murmured Raff, and sank to sleep again. As this could mean nothing but that he had buried the guilders there, Hans and his mother, when the house was quiet, dug all about the tree in the frozen ground that night, but with no reward—perhaps because the magic word *skates* was not mentioned. At least, when Annie Bouman came next day to talk over the skating-race and heard the story, she stamped on the ground twice at the back of the cottage, and said: "If I were a fairy god-mother, now, I would say, 'Open, earth, and show the treasure!'" She looked very bright and pretty as she said it, and her skates were hanging around her neck; so, for one reason or the other, Hans suddenly remembered that ten years ago there had been another willow-tree in just that place, but it had been cut down because it shaded the potatoes too much.

Of course you see how the story is coming out. Of course Hans and his mother dug again. Of course the treasure was there, and now every need of the dear father could be supplied without asking or accepting help from any one, however kind.

The skating race was run next day, and that very morning Hans secured steady work at wood-carving, from Peter van Holp's father. The blaze of sunshine on the Brinkers was now so intense that they almost had to put up their parasols to keep it off, for little Gretel—little yellow-haired, blue-eyed

Gretel—won the race and secured the silver skates, which did indeed have bells, in spite of what Voostenwalbert Schimmelpenninck had said.

Gretel was the fleetest sprite of a girl that ever skated: Dame Brinker and Hans had long known it, and now everybody saw it for himself. From that hour none despised her. Goose-girl or not, Gretel stood acknowledged Queen of the Skaters.

From that hour, too, whether it was skate-magic or not, everything went well with the Brinkers. The father recovered, the mother's life was no longer all toil and trouble, Gretel went to school every day, and Hans—this is the most wonderful magic of all—Hans was taken by the great Dr. Boekman to bring up as a pupil in surgery, and it was all on account of his honest eyes, his skillful hands, his fine scholarship, and his ready helpfulness when the doctor came to his father that winter night.

At least, that is what the doctor said: but we, who know that Hans and the great man were both on skates when they first met on the canal, may think that skate-magic had something to do with it.

# ALICE IN WONDERLAND*

HERE is a good old English singing game, called The Muffin Man, which many children know. John dances up to Jane, for instance, singing gayly, "Oh, do you know the Muffin Man, Who lives in Drury Lane?"

Jane immediately answers in song that she has the pleasure of his acquaintance, and the two take hands and run off to ask if Tommy has ever met him. It appears that Tommy knows him well, so the three trip away to inquire of Mary, who replies that he has long been one of her friends. So it goes on until everybody on the playground has been questioned and has joined the tradesman's friendly circle, and at last there is a triumphant burst of song, all the players proclaiming at once:

*Everybody* knows the Muffin Man
Who lives in Drury Lane.

If you played the same game with "Alice in Wonderland," in almost any schoolyard in this country, only a few boys and girls would be left out of the magic circle: but those unfortunate few have their rights and must be told of all the adorably funny things that happened to Alice, and of all the adorably funny Alices that happened to the things. I don't know which way it was, really. Perhaps it was a little of both.

Alice, you must know, was an adventurous young person, much more so than the heroines of the ordinary fairy tales, for when they wandered away from home it was generally because they were forced to do so, while Alice deliberately made up her mind to travel, and Did It!

*Lewis Carroll's work was originally entitled *Alice's Adventures in Wonderland*.

Mr. Lewis Carroll, who is responsible for Alice and her journeyings in Wonderland, spoke of her as a "dream-child," and her adventures are really like the dreams we sometimes have on restless nights.

The adventures began, of course, with the White Rabbit in Alice's garden. If she had not seen him hurrying by, looking at his watch and saying to himself: "Oh, dear! Oh, dear! I shall be too late!" and if she had not been "burning with curiosity" to know where he was going, she would not have followed him down the large rabbit-hole under the hedge. She did it, though, quite fearlessly, and never once did she consider how she was to get back if she did not fancy the place where she landed.

Alice fell . . . and fell . . . and fell—not at all frightened, you know, but rather astonished that anybody could fall so long and not get there, wherever *there* might be. The hole was rather like the deepest of deep wells, reaching down to China, or thereabouts, and it appeared to be lined with cupboards holding maps and books and orange marmalade and that kind of thing. She fell so long and so slowly that she began to get rather sleepy and to think of her cat, Dinah, and wonder if any one would remember to give her the usual saucer of milk at tea time.

She was beginning to nod and yawn as she fell, and to say drowsily to herself, "Dinah'll miss me very much tonight," when CRASH! she landed on a heap of dry leaves.

She wasn't a bit hurt, and she leaped to her feet just in time to see the White Rabbit disappearing down a long passage, and to hear him say, "Oh, my ears and whiskers, how late it is getting!"

What could Alice, or any other child, do but run after him when she had traveled so long without any satisfaction to her "burning curiosity"? She ran fast and she ran far, but not so fast as he, and at last she found herself in a long, low hall, with doors all around it, but all of them locked.

Of course Alice wanted to get out at once—everybody wants to get out when he is locked in and to get in when he is locked out—and, looking about the hall, she saw a golden key on a glass table.  She tried the key in all the doors, but it would not fit any of them until at last she found a little door, only about fifteen inches high, partly hidden by a low curtain.  The key easily opened this door, and, looking through it as she sat on the floor, Alice saw a wonderful garden and a fountain spraying rainbow lights among the flowers.

She longed to see the garden closer; but she was far too big to go through the door, and gazing helplessly about the room again, she saw on that same glass table a little bottle of liquid, and around the neck of the bottle a paper, saying, DRINK ME! in large letters.

Alice was so excited she thought she must try it, and, oh, the taste of it was simply lovely—"a sort of mixed flavor of cherry-tart, custard, pineapple, roast turkey, toffy, and buttered toast."

It was scarcely swallowed when, much to her surprise, she began to shut up like a telescope, and in a few moments she was only ten inches high and just big enough to go through the door.  But alas! she had laid the key back on the table when she took the bottle, and now it was as much out of her reach as the housetop is to you.  It *was* annoying, and what was she to do? She tried to climb up the legs of the table, but they were too slippery.  Then she saw a little cake on the floor marked, EAT ME! in letters made of currants.

She ate, first slowly then quickly, and in a moment her head knocked against the ceiling!  But now she was again too big to go through the door, and, though she had the key, she could only see into the garden by lying down on the floor with her head on one side and peeping with one eye.  She began to cry at this, and to cry so hard that she made a pool of tears four inches deep.

She was still crying when the White Rabbit, aggravating creature, pattered through the passage, muttering to himself, "Oh, the Duchess, the Duchess! Oh, won't she be savage if I've kept her waiting!" He didn't see Alice, and when she spoke he was so startled that he dropped the fan and white gloves he was carrying. It was a good thing, too, for Alice picked them up, and while she was fanning herself she noticed that she was shrinking again, and if she hadn't laid the fan down that very moment, who knows but she would have shrunk out of sight altogether!

"I never was so small as this before!" she cried, "and it's too bad!" At these words her foot slipped and, splash! she was up to her chin in salt water. Yes, it was—you may not believe it, but it truly was—the pool of her own tears. Of course it isn't surprising that she exclaimed, "How queer everything is today!" Just then she heard something splashing about on the other side of the pool, and she swam across, thinking it might be a walrus or a hippopotamus. You see, she'd forgotten how small she had grown, but she remembered it quickly enough when she saw that the splashing creature was only a little Mouse!

Now, Alice was courageous, adventurous, wide-awake, and rational; but she was not tactful, which word means, I suppose, trying to be agreeable and not to bring up subjects likely to be unpleasant to other people. Of course Alice was glad to see the Mouse, who was the only homelike thing she had met since she landed: but *why* should she have begun to talk to him about her cat, Dinah, and what a good mouser she was, and about a small terrier she knew, and how splendid he was at killing rats? No wonder the Mouse grew pale and trembled and swam to the shore. But Alice went, too, for the pool was quite crowded by this time, a Duck and a Dodo, a Lory and an Eaglet, all having unexpectedly fallen into the pool.

This was the first large assembly that Alice attended in Wonderland, and it was such a wet one that the Mouse offered to recite a History lesson, which he said he knew from experience would dry anybody up. Unfortunately, though, it did not have the expected effect; so the Dodo suggested a "Caucus-race." Now, Alice had never heard of a Caucus-race, and asked what it was, whereupon the Dodo very wisely answered that the best way to explain a thing was to do it, and he marked out a course on the floor, setting the members of the party along it, here and there. Everybody began running when he liked, and left off when he liked, and everybody got a prize, which Alice gave from a box of candy she had in her pocket and of which there was just enough to go around. The Mouse quickly saw that Alice had no prize, and mentioned it to the Dodo, who, on hearing that she also had a thimble in her pocket, ordered it out and presented it to her with a fine speech, while everybody cheered.

It was a lovely party, but Alice again forgot to be tactful, and began to talk about Dinah and how capital she was at catching birds, and would as soon eat a bird as look at it! It was only a moment after that when the whole assembly disappeared, and Alice, much surprised at the effect of her words, was left alone again.

Directly afterwards she found a Mushroom in a wood where she was wandering, and, stretching up to look at the top, saw upon it a Blue Caterpillar with his arms folded, quietly smoking a long pipe. He was a disagreeable Caterpillar, very contrary-minded and quite rude; but he gave Alice a good deal of sensible advice. She consulted him as to how she might regain a reasonable size, saying, in her usual unfortunate way, that three inches was such a wretched height to be!

As that was exactly the Blue Caterpillar's height, no wonder that his feelings were hurt, and that he dropped off the mushroom and began to crawl away at once.  He did mumble as he went, "One side will make you grow taller, and the other side shorter," and Alice concluded that he must be talking about the Mushroom.  She promptly ate a bit off one side, and crack! her chin hit her foot: she nibbled a piece off the other, and her head went soaring skyward.

You see, it's no trick at all to change your size when you have something handy to sip or to nibble, and if we could find the right things, I think we ought to keep them about us.  There's many a time when it would be pleasant to be able to slip out of the keyhole, and equally agreeable to wander about, breathing the air in the tree tops.

Alice, having now established herself at what she considered a proper size, decided to enter a house about four feet high that appeared near by, and there, seated on a three-legged stool in the kitchen with a baby in her lap, she found the Duchess, the very Duchess that the White Rabbit had talked about.  There was no one else present but the Cook, who was putting too much pepper in the soup, and a large Cat that sat on the rug and grinned from ear to ear.  It appears that it was a Cheshire Cat, and that they always grin. No; I don't know why. Perhaps because it is so pleasant in Cheshire.

The Duchess hadn't the manners that we associate with a lady of high degree, and she promptly told her visitor that she didn't know much—which was true, but rather impolite; and she finally threw the baby into Alice's arms and told her to take care of it as she had an engagement to play croquet with the Queen.  She did say one important thing, though, before she disappeared, which was (and I hope she didn't intend it for Alice!):

"If everybody minded their own business, the world would go round a deal faster than it does."

Alice immediately walked away with the baby, which turned out to be a Pig, and which jumped down from her arms, grunting, and soon Alice met the Cheshire Cat again, sitting on the branch of a tree and grinning. The Cat met her several times, always appearing suddenly and disappearing in sections, as it were, beginning with the tail and ending with the grin, which hung in the air after he had gone.

"I've often seen a Cat without a grin," thought Alice; "but never before a grin without a Cat.  It's the most curious thing I ever saw in all my life!"

He certainly was a curious Cat, but we must remember in his favor that without him Alice would never have known where to find the Mad Hatter, the Mad March Hare, and the Dormouse, and never would have been invited (or invited herself) to the Mad Tea-party.

It was the Mad Hatter who told Alice—they all were so rude—that her hair wanted cutting, and who asked her the famous conundrum: "Why is a Raven like a writing-desk?" which Alice couldn't answer, but perhaps you can.

It was the Dormouse, though, who, half-asleep all the time, told the story about the three little sisters who were learning to draw, and who "drew everything that began with an M, such as mouse-trap, and the moon, and memory, and much of a muchness."  How *do* you draw "much of a muchness," I wonder!

When the March Hare and the Hatter began to try and squeeze the Dormouse into the teapot, Alice walked away, quite disgusted, and directly she found herself on the Queen's croquet ground, which was hard by that beautiful garden she had seen when she first came to Wonderland.

Alice was looking about her, admiring everything, when a company of soldiers and courtiers came in sight, escorting the King and Queen of Hearts and their guests, among whom was the White Rabbit.  After the usual intro-

*The Little Lame Prince*
PAGE 56

*Heidi*
PAGE 65

Mowgli, in *The Jungle Book*

*Rebecca of Sunnybrook Farm*
PAGE 92

ductions, Alice was invited to play croquet, but the game was difficult, not to say impossible, for the balls were live hedgehogs, the mallets live flamingoes, and the wickets, the accommodating soldiers who arched themselves in proper shape and stood on their hands and feet. The Queen, too, who was a lady of high temper, ordered a person's head cut off if he made the least mistake, so it was not long before the royal lady herself, the King, and Alice were the only players left, and Alice felt so uncomfortable that she was very glad when the Queen suggested that she go and ask the Gryphon to take her to see the Mock Turtle and hear his history.

The Mock Turtle was the most curious creature that Alice had met in all her travels, though he was very highly educated, for he had been to school every day in his youth and had learned "Reeling and Writhing and the different branches of Arithmetic—Ambition, Distraction, Uglification, and Derision." Add to this that he had been taught "Drawling, Stretching, and Fainting in Coils," and you can see how improving his society must have been.

The Gryphon had been his schoolmate, and it was he who told Alice that in his time they did lessons ten hours the first day, nine hours the next, and so on, and when Alice said that it seemed a strange plan, explained that that was the reason they were called lessons, because they *lessened* from day to day.

Then the Gryphon and the Mock Turtle kindly told Alice about the Lobster Quadrille and gave her the directions for the first figure, as follows:

"Form two lines along the seashore, seals, turtles, salmon, and so on; then, when you've cleared the jelly-fish all out of the way, you advance twice, each with a lobster as a partner; set to partners, change lobsters, and retire in same order. Then you throw the lobsters as far out to sea as you can, swim after them, turn a somersault in the water, change lobsters again, and back to land."

Alice thought it must be a very pretty dance, and was going to try it with her new friends when a voice was heard in the distance crying, "The trial's beginning, the trial's beginning!" and everybody ran off to the Queen's garden again.

It was the trial, it appeared, of the Knave of Hearts, who was accused of having stolen some tarts that the Queen had made for the King. Of course everybody was present and all were grouped about the King and Queen on their gorgeous thrones.

But, oh, it was such a confused trial that you could hardly make out what it was all about. The jurors wrote down all the evidence on their slates, and some had no pencils, and some couldn't spell. Everybody gave evidence—the Hatter, the Dormouse, the March Hare, the Duchess's Cook, though nothing of what they said had anything to do with the case, and Alice, who had just then unexpectedly begun to grow to her natural size, felt like a giantess when she was called up as the next witness.

She upset all the jurors in the jury-box when she went to her place, and had to pick them up again before she could tell the judge that she didn't know anything whatever about the business. After that everything was more confused than ever, and it may have been because Alice had grown more discerning as she grew larger; but at last she saw plainly what she had long suspected, and cried out in the face of a perfectly nonsensical verdict: "Who cares for you? You're nothing but a pack of cards!"

"Dear me," you say; "how very tactless!" Yes, it was; and you will not be surprised to hear that the whole pack immediately rose up into the air and came flying down upon her, furiously; nor will you be surprised, perhaps, to hear that this is the end of the story, for Alice gave a little scream of fright and anger, tried to beat the cards off and immediately woke up, saying to herself, "Why, what a curious dream I've had!"

I'm not sure that the Dream, or the Story, has any moral, you know; but if it has, it is what the Duchess said on another occasion:

"Never imagine yourself not to be otherwise than what it might appear to others that what you were or might have been was not otherwise than what you had been would have appeared to them to be otherwise."

# THE LITTLE LAME PRINCE

CHRISTENING parties seem to have been very difficult to manage in the days of Fairy Royalty. Either no King and Queen of that time ever made out a proper visiting list, or no edition of Who's Who in Fairyland had yet been issued. The Court Chamberlain, who sent out the cards for the occasion, always managed to make some mistake—either inviting some one who should never have been there, or leaving out one whose presence was absolutely necessary.

It was the idea, as I have understood, to invite just as many Kind, Benevolent, and Good-tempered Fairies as Unkind, Malignant, and Ill-tempered ones, and then the one party offset the other, so that when old Fairy Wormwood wished the new-born babe a hasty temper, for instance, kind Fairy Honey-dew might wish him a forgiving disposition.

If this balance of guests were not maintained, the infant turned out either so good that it was hardly possible for an ordinary mortal to live with him, or so naughty that nobody could endure him at all. Sometimes, of course, the disaster that ensued was physical, not mental or spiritual, and so it was with Prince Dolor, the Little Lame Prince, whose fairy godmother arrived at the party too late. Being lame herself, and obliged to use a crutch, she lagged behind the other magic ladies, and so could give nothing to bless when a wicked enchantress cursed the child.

You understand, of course, that this fairy christening-party I have been talking about was invisible to mortal eyes and took place before the royal one which everybody saw. But perhaps I'd better begin at the beginning of the story, as Miss Mulock tells it in her book called "The Little Lame Prince," and then it will all be quite clear to you.

The King and Queen of Nomansland, a very large and populous country, had been waiting ever since they were married, and that was ten long years, for a son and heir to wear the crown and succeed them in power. I should tell you, too, that the King had a younger brother who did not care how long they waited, and was quite willing that the wished-for son should never appear at all, for in that case he would wear the crown himself.

It happened, however, very much against this royal gentleman's will, that a baby boy was born at last to the happy King and Queen, and that he was the most beautiful child ever seen, not only in Nomansland but in the entire round world.

When the people of the country heard the news, they nearly went wild with joy; it was like Thanksgiving, Christmas, New Year's, and Independence Day all rolled into one: cannon were fired, bells rang incessantly, and everybody feasted everybody else. The King's brother, now the baby's devoted uncle, of course, feasted with the rest, and if he did not have much appetite, everybody was too excited to notice it.

The christening was to be a very grand affair. All the important people were asked from all neighboring countries, and four and twenty godfathers and godmothers were chosen with care as persons who would be useful to his little Royal Highness should he ever need powerful friends in the future. It didn't seem at all likely that he would—but then, you never can tell!

There was one cloud and only one upon the whole affair, and that was that Queen Dolorez, the little Prince's mother, was ill and had never risen from her bed in the whole six weeks since he was born. He was brought to her in his christening robes, and she kissed him and blessed him; but she was too weak to rise, and the ceremony must go on without her. She hoped that the baby would be good, and that everything would pass off well; and then she patiently turned her face to her windows and looked out toward the Beautiful Mountains where she was born.

The little Prince's nurse, a strong peasant woman, was not thought grand enough to carry him on such a day, and so he was entrusted to the arms of a young lady of rank who, whatever her other accomplishments, could not have known much about carrying babies, for she stumbled and let him fall just at the foot of the marble staircase.

That was the beginning of the whole trouble, of course; but if the little Prince cried out, nobody heard it for the silver trumpets were blowing so loud a strain. The high-born damsel picked the baby up again—a soft, white bundle of frills and laces, and the procession moved on, two and two, earls and countesses, dukes and duchesses, to the cathedral where his godmothers and godfathers in baptism each gave him a name.

When the ceremony was over and the procession was about to return to the palace, a little old woman all dressed in gray, with gray hair and a gray hooded cloak, appeared among the guests, and drawing near the high-born damsel who held the child, she whispered: "Take care! Don't let him fall again!" The culprit started and flushed angrily, for she hoped that no one had seen what she had done, and she ordered the little old woman in gray to leave at once and not come near her royal charge.

"Oh, but I must kiss him!" said the little gray woman, and leaning on her stick she stretched up and gave the baby three kisses. "And I shall name him, too," she cried; "for I am his fairy godmother, and I name him Prince Dolor, in memory of his mother, Queen Dolorez."

"In *memory* of his mother?" cried the courtiers. "Why, the Queen is living, still!" and they tried to drive away the little woman; but she melted into nothing, like a cloud, and in a moment only the tap of her stick could be heard.

It appeared, however, that she knew what had happened far better than they, and before the baby could be laid in the arms of his own nurse again, the solemn tolling of the bells proclaimed that indeed the Queen had passed away.

Of course the King was very sorrowful, and for long he did not care to see the little Prince at all. So there was no one to heed that the poor child was greatly changed from the plump and rosy baby of his christening-day, and although the nurse must have seen that his little legs grew thinner and weaker, no doubt she was afraid to mention it.

By and by the King asked to see his son and heir, once a week, at least; and, after a long time, when Dolor was more than two years old, his father one day noticed that he could not stand upon his legs, but merely crept upon the floor or dragged himself by his arms from chair to chair.

The King was by this time so ill and so melancholy that he might not have noticed it even then, save that his brother, the wicked uncle, pointed it out. Then doctors were sent for, and everything possible was done for the poor little Prince, but nothing was of any avail. The King's heart now seemed broken altogether, and he pined away and died.

Then the wicked uncle was appointed Regent of the kingdom, and swore solemnly to perform all his duties and to take all care of his little lame nephew who was now, though such a baby, the rightful King of the Country. He did take all care of him, as you will see, but in such a way as I hope will never be taken of you!

The Regent-Uncle, it seems, had seven fine sons, all strong and with straight legs, and he thought that in time one of them would make a much better King than little Dolor; so he went to the Council one day and made a speech in which he said that Dolor's health required a change of climate, and that he was about to send him to the Beautiful Mountains for a time. The Council agreed to this plan, and nobody was much surprised when, not long after, it was learned that the poor delicate little fellow had died upon the journey.

Of course, you know that he had not died, or the story of the little lame prince would have been too short to put in a book. The Regent-Uncle was wicked enough, but not so wicked as to order the child killed; he sent him instead to a desert land beyond the Beautiful Mountains, where no one ever traveled, and gave him as his future home a great round tower of brickwork, called Hopeless Tower, one hundred feet high, with neither doors nor windows until near the top.

Prince Dolor was sent there in charge of a follower of the Regent, who was both deaf and dumb, and so could be trusted not to tell secrets; and with them went a woman who was to be the child's nurse, and who was under sentence of death, but who would be permitted to live so long as she kept the child alive.

When they reached Hopeless Tower, they saw a chain hanging half-way down from the top, and to this the deaf-mute fitted a ladder that he carried with him and that could be taken apart and put together like a puzzle. By this means the nurse and her charge climbed to a little house of four rooms that had been fitted up for them in the very top of the tower, and then the deaf-mute rode away, it being understood that he was to return once a month with provisions.

The little house was comfortable enough—rather like a nest in a tree-top—and there were plenty of picture-books and playthings, so the Prince was not unhappy, and the nurse was not so wicked a woman but that she soon learned to love and take great care of her charge. New books were brought him every time the deaf-mute came, and he soon learned to read, and so had a new way of amusing himself.

As Dolor grew older, however, he grew lonely and longed for some one to talk to and to explain things to him. The nurse had been forbidden to tell him who he really was, and though she called him "Prince" and "Royal Highness," those words meant nothing to him. He was sitting alone one day, looking out of a window-slit in the tower, when he sighed and said aloud:

"Oh, I do want some one to love me and be kind to me—oh, dreadfully, dreadfully!"

At that moment the tap of a cane was heard, and there stood a little gray lady, with gray hair and the sweetest smile in the world.

"My dear little boy," she cried, "I am your fairy godmother, and I have been waiting and waiting to come to you: but I could not come until you said you wanted me. Now I will come whenever you call."

Then she took the poor lamb in her arms and hugged him and kissed him, and said she had brought him a present—a wonderful traveling-cloak, so that now he could go about every day and see the world.

"But I cannot walk!" cried Dolor. "How can I use a traveling-cloak?"

"This is a different kind of cloak from any you know," said his godmother, smiling; "and I will show you how to use it."

She then gave him a little bundle that could be made small enough to hide in his pocket, showed him how to open it, to sit on it, and what words to say when he wanted to travel, and what when he wanted to return. The words were very important, and you must learn them if you should ever have such a cloak:

### Charm to Travel

Abra-ca-dabra, tum, tum, tum!
Cloak of the Traveler, Bird become!

Carry me fast and carry me far,
Far as the flight of the Evening Star!
When I am weary, backward come,
Abra-ca-dabra, tum, tum, tum!

### Charm to Return

Abra-ca-dabra, tum, tum, ti,
Carry me back, from the far blue sky,
Back to my tower, my room, my bed,
Cover me up for a sleepy-head!

Now about the traveling-cloak, in case you should want to make one. Ask your mother for a piece of old material—any kind will do—and cut a circle out of it whose diameter (that's the width across, you know) shall be double your own height. Cut a hole in the middle of the circle, big enough to put your head through, and if the garment falls to your feet when you put it on, it is properly shaped. Now lay it out flat on the floor, and if the hole you have made shuts up immediately with a click, and the edge of the cloak turns up a few inches all around to make a kind of fence—then you may leap into the middle of it, sit there cross-legged, as Dolor did, say the Travel Charm, and, whisk! off you go!*

That traveling-cloak was the very best present the Little Lame Prince had ever had; and when he was troubled with the doldrums or the fidgets in the morning, he used to make it ready at once and sail away from the top of the tower. His nurse never missed him, for his godmother, who knew the secret of many charms, used to make a figure just like him out of moonshine and put it in his chair while he was gone. Of course, while sailing high in the air on his wonderful cloak, he could not see things on the earth very plainly; so his godmother also gave him a pair of gold spectacles through which he could watch even the ants crawling down below; and once she changed

---

*Of course, it's really your imagination that carries you to all these faraway and fascinating places.

herself into a magpie and went with him on the cloak and explained the world to him.

Knowing no other boys and seeing no other people, the Prince had never realized how helpless he was until one day while traveling through the air he saw a shepherd lad on the meadows playing with his dog, and the Prince noticed how light and swift the lad was, and how he bounded over the grass. Thereafter, for a long time, poor Dolor did not wish to go abroad, and sat sadly in his tower, thinking of his misfortunes. One day it suddenly occurred to him as he mused that his attendant always called him "Prince," and he said to her, thoughtfully: "Nurse, tell me—shall I ever be a king?"

Now the miserable woman had been threatened with death if she ever told the boy who he really was: but she had grown to love him, and she wondered if writing the information on a slate would be breaking her oath. Anyway, she did it, and wrote hurriedly, "You *are* a king," and then in a few sentences she told him all his history. "We shall die here in this lonely tower," she added, with a burst of tears, "unless you can get out into the world and fight for your rights like a man."

It was not long after this day when the Prince, awaking one morning, heard no answer to his calls, and, making his way as best he could about the little house found it empty. All was in order, and food was set, but his attendant had vanished; and, looking down to the base of the tower, he saw the marks of horses' hoofs, and a scattered litter of hay and corn. The deaf-mute had evidently come as usual and had carried away his nurse—but to what purpose? Was the Prince deserted? Was he to die alone? Or had they gone back to Nomansland to tell his subjects he was living?

Dolor was fifteen years old now and full of courage although so crippled, and he resolved to take care of himself as best he could and never to lose hope of rescue. The days went slowly by, and at last, leaning from a window-slit, he heard the sound of a silver trumpet—such as those that had blown on his christening-day.

All had happened that he had fancied possible. The Regent-Uncle was dead, and the people of Nomansland had come to offer him his rightful crown. They fell upon their knees before him, and he answered their plea, saying, "Yes, if you desire it, I will be your king; and I will do my best to make my people happy."

So the Little Lame Prince, now a king in robe and crown, went away to his palace in Nomansland; and as he grew in years and wisdom, so he governed his kingdom more and more wisely. His little gray godmother never deserted him, and whenever he went to the room where the Queen had died, and looked out on the Beautiful Mountains, his godmother came to him and gave him good counsel.

When his years grew heavy upon him, he trained a young cousin as his successor; and when this task was done he told his people that he was aweary and that it was time for him to go on a long journey. They prayed that he would not leave them; but he answered no word—only took from his clothing a shabby little bundle, opened it, murmured something they could not understand, and was away into the air!

"Whither he went, or who went with him, it is impossible to say. But I myself believe that his godmother took him on his traveling-cloak to the Beautiful Mountains."

# HEIDI, THE ALPINE ROSE

THE very breath of the mountains is in Johanna Spyri's story of "Heidi," and as we read it we see the snow-capped summits of the higher Alps, the green summer slopes of the Alm, where Heidi's grandfather lived, and the brilliant flowers bordering the streams. We hear the wind in the fir trees, and the tinkle of goat-bells; we smell healthful odors of fresh leaves, spicy herbs and grasses, and, though we may never have tasted black bread, goats' milk, or goats' milk cheese, our mouths fairly water as we hear about them and watch Heidi at her simple meals.

We first see the five-year-old child in the story as she trudges up the Alm, one of the lower peaks of the Alps, beside her aunt Dete. She is scarcely more than a baby, but strong, active, intelligent, and more than commonly independent and self-helpful, because she is an orphan, without brothers or sisters, and has tumbled about with very little care, almost since her birth. Her aunt Dete has had a more or less unwilling charge of her up to this time, and now, having secured for herself a good place with a family in Frankfort, she is taking her little niece to her unknown grandfather who lives alone in a hut far up the mountain.

At the village of Dörfli, Aunt Dete had fallen in with an old neighbor who was curious to know not only where she was going with the child, but all that had happened since they last met, and they walked together up the steep path, talking so busily that Heidi was quite forgotten. The neighbor was on her way to Peter, the goatherd's hut, to see Peter's blind grandmother about some spinning, and it was not until she had entered the little shelter which stood about half-way between Dörfli and the top of the Alm that Dete realized that Heidi was not to be seen. "She must have met Peter, the goatherd, and be climbing up with him," she said to herself; and she stood still and watched for their appearance. It was Peter's business through the spring, summer, and early autumn to collect the goats in Dörfli, drive them up the Alm where they might feed on the thick grass and herbs, tend them during the day, and return them at night to the village. Only in winter, when he went to school, did he have time to play with other children, for, though he was only eleven years old, his day's work was from sun to sun. Meeting little Heidi trudging along by herself as he drove his goats up the mountain, he had at once made friends with her and was overjoyed to hear that she was on her way to live with the "Alm-uncle," as everybody in the village called Heidi's grandfather.

The path was steep, the sun began to grow warm, and Heidi looked enviously at Peter's thin shirt and trousers and his bare feet. She herself wore new shoes and woolen stockings, a heavy red shawl, and over her every-day dress her Sunday one, which Aunt Dete thought would be easiest carried in that way. The weight was not to be borne—no, she would not bear it; and sitting down on a rock, the child stripped off shoes, stockings, and both dresses, and, wrapping them all neatly in the red shawl, she skipped up the rocks after Peter in her petticoat, stretching her bare arms to the breeze in great delight.

No wonder Aunt Dete could not believe her eyes when she saw the children coming, nor that she screamed, "Where are your clothes, you naughty child, and your new shoes, and the beautiful stockings I knitted you?" Heidi turned and calmly pointed down the mountain where the red package could plainly be seen, though at a good distance away. "You careless little thing!" stormed Dete. "Now how shall we get it, and I take you up the Alm and get back to the village before dark? Run, Peter, and bring it to me."

"I am late already," said Peter, slowly.

"Run, and I'll give you this," coaxed Dete, showing him a bright five-cent piece.

At once Peter was off like a shot and was back again, the five-cent piece in his pocket, before they had had time to miss him. He offered to carry the bundle as far as the Alm-uncle's, for he was going there, anyway, to get the uncle's goats; so the three climbed on together, Heidi frisking along as nimbly as the four-footed creatures of the herd.

Grandfather's hut was on the crest of a great rock, exposed to all the winds that blew. Behind it were three tall fir trees, and green grass and herbage stretched up the slope as far as the great bare rocks of the mountain itself. On a bench in front of the door sat Grandfather, smoking; and though he had not seen Heidi since the death of his son and daughter-in-law, when the child had been but a year old, he recognized Dete as she climbed, and surmised what might be the object of her call.

A disappointed, embittered old man, his son dead, his life a failure, he had left the village and its people and betaken himself to this mountain shelter, with only his goats for companions both summer and winter. Yet his heart was still warm and still in the right place, and he felt it beat when the child's wild little figure ran toward him with outstretched hands, crying: "Grandfather! Grandfather! It's Heidi!"

Before he listened to Dete's breathless explanation of why she was there, and why she had brought Heidi, and why she could not take charge of her any longer, and how it was now his duty to do something for the child, the Alm-uncle dispatched Peter on his way with the goats, and then set himself to attend to the question before him.   The confused torrent of words had not long poured forth before the old man said, sternly, "The upshot of the matter is that you don't want any further trouble with the child, and want to turn her over to me."   Yes; that was it, Dete confessed.   "And you are quite willing to leave her up here on a mountain-top, without any playmates, and with an old man who knows little about children?"

Yes; the aunt was quite willing; and if anything happened, the blame would be on the Alm-uncle's own head, for she would have none of it.

"Very well, then; go your way as soon as you will, and the sooner the better," growled the old man.   "Give me the child's clothes and be off with you."

Heidi had listened to part of this conversation, but had soon hurried off to look at the great fir trees and to hear them sing in the wind.   She knew already that the Alm was a place after her own heart, and she watched Aunt Dete hurrying down the mountain path, with not one sigh of regret.   Then she ran to the front of the hut where her grandfather still sat, lost in thought, and said, with decision, "I should like to see the house, now."

The old man looked at her with a half-smile, and said, rising, "Come, then, and bring your bundles."

"Oh, no," said Heidi; "I don't want the dresses any more.   I want to go about like Peter."

"You shall, then," said her grandfather; "but bring your clothes anyway, and put them in the closet," and they entered the hut together.

It held but one room, with an outbuilding for the goats; and the fireplace was in one corner, a bed in another, and a table, a chair, a three-legged stool, and a cupboard formed the remaining furniture.   Heidi ran to the cupboard at once and thrust her bundles as far back as possible, seeing at the same time that bread and cheese and meat were on one of the shelves, knives and forks and plates on another, and what looked like Grandfather's clean shirts and stockings on a third.

Her bright eyes ran quickly about the room. "Where shall I sleep?" she asked. "Oh, wherever you like," was the reply. In one corner of the apartment was a ladder, and up this Heidi ran like a squirrel, finding above a loft filled with sweet-smelling hay, its one round window looking down the green slopes to the valley below and the village of Dörfli.

In great delight, Heidi heaped up a bed and a pillow of hay by the window, and called out, "I have a lovely bed, Grandfather; but I need a sheet. There are always sheets on a bed." The old man soon appeared with a heavy piece of linen, which he spread carefully over bed and pillow. "That is nice, Grandfather," said Heidi; "but there is no coverlet. When one goes to bed, one always creeps between the sheets and the coverlet."

"True, my child. I will get one for you"; and in a minute the old man was down and up the ladder again with a heavy linen sack which he laid in place.

"That is exactly right," said Heidi, approvingly; "and now I will go to bed."

"But will there not be supper?" asked Grandfather.

Supper! That did sound good, for Heidi had had nothing since her hasty breakfast, and now it was late afternoon, so she eagerly watched the fire kindled and the milk set on to heat, and while her grandfather toasted a great piece of cheese to a golden brown, she laid the table, brought the bread, and dragged up the three-legged stool for herself.

Grandfather soon came with the steaming milk and the cheese, pushed up his chair for her to use as a table, and filled her mug to the brim. Oh, it was good; and how delicious the warm, soft cheese on the thick piece of black bread that Grandfather had cut for her!

The feast was only just over when Peter's whistle was heard, and down the slope the goats came capering, two slender, beautiful creatures separating themselves from the herd and coming to Grandfather's hand for salt. The white one, Heidi learned, was called Schwänli (Swanling), and the brown one Bärli (Bearling); and she followed them into their pen, saw them milked and fed and bedded, and loved everything she saw. Then there was her own bed on the sweet hay, with a long look first from the little round window of the loft; and whoever had seen Alm-uncle climb the ladder twice during the night to assure himself of the child's repose would have known that she was secure in his charge.

Next day was a long delight, for she was told that she might go up the Alm with Peter and the goats, was given her luncheon, and the lad was told that he was to milk Swanling for her when noontime came.

Oh, the flowers up the mountain! Oh, the fresh, clear winds! Oh, the darling goats, all of whose names and dispositions she learned from Peter! Oh, the good, good food, and the wonderful sunset when sky and rocks turned golden and rosy red! Never was there a happier little girl, and Peter and Grandfather seemed as happy as she.

Whenever the sun shone, she went up the Alm with Swanling and Bearling, and learned about Peter's mother, and how hard she worked, and his poor, blind grandmother, and how she still could spin; and between them they all managed to earn their poor food and clothing.

So passed the summer; and when the first snow fell, the goats came up the Alm no more, and Peter went to school in Dörfli, although, as he confided to Heidi, it was no use, for he could not learn to read, and he advised her never to try, for nobody but a witch could remember what those little black marks on the paper meant.

Several times during the long, cold winter Grandfather wrapped Heidi warmly, put her on his sled, and coasted with her down to visit Peter's blind grandmother, while he went to Dörfli to sell the cheeses he had made from the milk of his goats.

So, happily passed the winter, another summer as delightful as the first, another winter still, and Heidi was nearly eight years old, and the minister climbed up from Dörfli one day to tell Grandfather that when cold weather came again he must bring the child to the village, for now she must go to school and to church.

The Alm-uncle would not agree, for both Heidi and he loved their lonely mountain-hut; but while he still pondered the matter, Aunt Dete surprisingly arrived and proposed a way out of the difficulty. A Mr. Sesemann, a rich merchant of Frankfort, had, it seemed, a little invalid daughter, unable to walk; and he wished to find a child-companion for her, to play with her and share her lessons. Aunt Dete had suggested Heidi, her suggestion had been adopted, and she had come to take away her most unwilling niece, who, although she was told she was to live in a wonderful house in great comfort and luxury, was broken-hearted at the prospect of leaving Grandfather, the beloved hut, the goats, and the free life of the mountain.

But of what use to sob and cry and pray to stay? Aunt Dete was determined. Grandfather agreed that she was right, Heidi must go to Frankfort and leave all she loved behind her, must even learn to read, perhaps; and the only consolation was that if everything about her was to be so grand, she might save all the white rolls served to her at table and send them back to the blind grandmother who could no longer eat the hard black bread.

Clara Sesemann, whose feeble limbs and wheeled chair were a source of great wonderment at first, was most loving and companionable, and her tutor was most anxious for Heidi to learn, but the mountain child was like a wild bird in a cage, beating her head furiously against the bars. She stifled for air, her clothing was too heavy, the carpets too thick, the food too rich, the beds too soft, and she would have cried for homesickness night and day had not the housekeeper sternly forbidden it.

By and by Heidi noted that Clara appeared to be no more intelligent than she in many ways, and yet she had mastered the art of reading; and then the child began to realize that there was a connection between those "little black marks on the paper," as Peter called them, and the stories Clara found in the picture-books. She would learn to read herself, and then when she went home she could read from the Bible and the hymn book to the old blind grandmother. The new knowledge, and the daily growing pile of white rolls in her closet, were all that reconciled her to city life; and when the housekeeper scolded her for an untidy child, and took the rolls away, she was inconsolable till Clara promised her she should have fresh ones when she went home.

To go home, to go home—that was all Heidi wanted; and at last the old doctor, called in to advise about the child's growing thinness and pallor, agreed that home would be her only cure. He even promised, and Mr. Sesemann agreed, that Clara should be sent up the Alm in summer-time, and they would see what mountain air would do for her case.

So, in charge of one of the servants, the happy Heidi was taken as far as Dörfli one morning, with warm, new clothing, a purse of money for herself, and a basket of white rolls and cakes for Peter's grandmother. Leaving her box in the village, she scampered up the steep path to Peter's hut, and soon the goodies were in grandmother's lap and her arms around the child's neck. But Heidi could not stay, no, not a minute; and, tossing her fine, feathered hat on the table, for she never should want it again, she was off up the mountain.

You can picture for yourself the joy with which her grandfather greeted her, the way in which Peter danced and shouted, and the prancing and capering of Swanling and Bearling. Perhaps you can see, too, Clara Sesemann on the Alm, by and by, in the long summer days, realize her growing strength, and know that soon she will be able to ramble among the Alpine grass and flowers as well as the goats themselves.

You may even be able to take a long look into the future and see Grandfather living in the village the very next winter, Heidi going to church and to school, Swanling and Bearling enjoying the advantages of a metropolis, and Peter slowly making up his mind to learn his letters.

Whether you can see them or not, all these things came true, and it is true, too, that there never was a wiser, sweeter, more industrious, more lovable village maiden than our little mountain Heidi grew to be as the years went by.

# MOWGLI

OULD you like to know how Mowgli, the man-cub, came to the wolf's lair in the jungle? Rudyard Kipling tells us in "The Jungle Book" that this was the way of it, and a strange happening it was, though not so strange, after all, as the welcome the cub received there.

Shere Khan, the lame Tiger, was out hunting that night and in the dark valley below Father Wolf could hear his dry, angry, singsong whine. "He hunts Man in the village," snarled Mother Wolf, "the Wicked One, and now the people will scour the jungle for him when he is far away and we and our children must run when the grass is set alight," and she looked down and nosed her four gray cubs.

Just then a frightful howl came from the lame Tiger and Father Wolf ran to the mouth of the cave to see what had happened.

"Shere Khan has had no more sense than to jump at a woodcutter's camp-fire, so he has burned his feet," growled Father Wolf, with a hoarse, barking laugh.

"Careful!" cried Mother Wolf, twitching one ear, "careful! Something is coming up-hill!"

Father Wolf crouched at the mouth of the cave and waited and in a moment he leaped up straight into the air for at least five feet, in sheer astonishment.

"Man!" he snapped. "A man's cub. Look!"

Directly in front of him, holding on by a low branch, stood a naked brown baby who could just walk—as soft and dimpled a little thing as ever

74

came to a wolf's cave at night. He looked up into Father Wolf's face and laughed.

"Is that a man's cub?" asked Mother Wolf, eagerly. "Bring it here. I have never seen one."

Father Wolf, who was used to handling his own cubs, took the baby up carefully in his great jaws and carried it to her side.

"Ahai! how little and how naked!" said Mother Wolf, softly. "See, he is pressing close to me and taking his dinner with the others! Was there ever a wolf before that could boast of a man's cub in her litter?"

"I have heard of it many times, but never saw it," answered Father Wolf. "See, he is altogether without hair and I could kill him with a touch of my paw, but he fears nothing."

At this moment Shere Khan's great head and burning eyes blocked the mouth of the cave. "Give me back the man's cub!" he growled. "The parents have fled and this is my quarry."

Father Wolf knew that the entrance to the cave was too small for the great Tiger to force his way in, so he was the bolder to cry out: "The Wolves are a free people and take orders from the Head of the Pack and not from any striped cattle killer. The man's cub is ours—to kill if we choose."

"Dogs! Do ye defy Shere Khan?" roared the Tiger, with a voice like thunder rolling.

Then Mother Wolf shook herself clear of her cubs and sprang forward, her eyes like two green moons in the darkness.

"The man's cub is mine!" she cried. "He shall not be killed. He shall live to run with the Pack and to hunt with the Pack and in the end, thou cruel hunter of naked cubs, he shall live to hunt *thee!*" and she glared with anger.

Shere Khan heard her, saw her fierce teeth and those of her mate, saw how little room there was for fighting and wisely backed out of the mouth of the cave, growling:

"We will see what the Pack will say to this fostering of man-cubs. The cub is mine and to my teeth he will come in the end, O bush-tailed thieves!"

The struggle was over and Father Wolf looked gravely at the panting Mother. "Wilt thou indeed keep the cub?" he asked. "It is true as Shere Khan says, he must be shown to the Pack."

"Keep him!" she gasped. "He came to us alone, hungry and unafraid. He lies with the others by my side. Assuredly we will keep him. Lie still, little frog! O thou Mowgli—for Mowgli, the Frog, will I call thee—the time will come as I have said, when thou wilt hunt Shere Khan as he has hunted thee."

So Mowgli became a member of the Wolf family, tumbled about the cave with the other cubs, shared their food and their training and though he had no thick coat of hair to protect him and often suffered from their half-playful, half-caressing bites, yet he loved his Gray Brothers and knew not yet that he was a man-cub or differed from the others in any way.

Once every month the Wolf Pack was accustomed to meet with their leader on a night of full moonlight and the time soon came for Mowgli and the other cubs to be taken to the meeting to face inspection by all the grown wolves, that they might be recognized and receive protection from Pack members when, by and by, they should go hunting alone.

The place of meeting was Council Rock where were many dens for hiding should occasion arise, and a hundred members were gathered there, with great gray Akela, the Lone Wolf, their leader, in the center. The Wolves sat about the circle with red, hanging tongues and blazing eyes and as Akela cried from time to time in a loud, monotonous voice, "Look well,

O wolves, look well! Ye know the Law," one or another would rise, trot about and smell and inspect the cubs that had been brought to the meeting.

Baloo, the sleepy brown bear who is the Wolf Schoolmaster and teaches the Law of the Jungle, was present, and so was Bagheera, the Black Panther, with his soft voice and down-soft fur, and a very good thing it was for Mowgli, as you will see, that both were there. When the little fellow was brought into the circle and sat laughing and playing with some bright pebbles, "so little and so naked," as Mother Wolf had said, both Baloo and Bagheera felt an instant impulse of love and protection for him.

There was much discussion among the Wolves as to whether a man-cub might justly be admitted to the Pack and as two members besides his parents must speak for him, Mowgli's fate seemed doubtful, more especially as Shere Khan behind a sheltering rock began to roar out again his rightful claims to his prey.

At last old Baloo rose up on his hind quarters and grunted: "I have no gift of words, but I speak the truth. There is no harm in a man's cub. Let him be admitted to the Pack and I will teach him."

"We need yet another," cried Akela. "Who speaks besides Baloo?"

Then Bagheera dropped softly as thistle-down into the circle, and his voice was like the dripping of wild honey. "Ye know," he purred, "that the Law of the Jungle says that the life of a cub may be paid with a price. I have a new-killed bullock not half a mile from here. Shall that be the price of the little Frog and he be admitted to the Pack? Speak, then!"

Now wolves are always hungry and the price pleased them, so they all howled at once, "Let him be accepted! Let him be accepted!" and tumbled down the hill to the bullock like a stream of water at the breaking of a dam.

So Mowgli was entered into the Seonee Wolf pack for the price of Bagheera's bull and on Baloo's good word and these two, with Kaa, the big

Rock Python, became his best and dearest friends in the jungle. Father and Mother Wolf and the four Gray Brothers were his own family, of course, and "Father Wolf taught him his business and the meaning of things in the jungle, till every rustle in the grass, every breath of the night air, every note of the owls above his head, every scratch of a bat's claws as it roosted for a while in a tree, and every splash of every little fish jumping in a pool, meant as much to him as the work of his office means to a business man."

Bagheera taught him how to climb trees carefully and yet boldly, and how to leap swiftly and soundlessly upon his prey and Baloo taught him where to find nuts and honey and above all, taught him the Laws of the Jungle and the hunting calls to give to the jungle people, to each one his proper greeting and his Magic Word.

Baloo, being wise and experienced and a schoolmaster by profession, knew much better than the wolves what a man-cub was and what he could do when grown, and Bagheera was even more experienced in the ways of men, for he had been born in captivity, in the cages of the King's Palace at Oodeypore and had broken his bars and escaped to the jungle.

Mother Wolf, when the little Frog sat by her as he grew older and pulled the long thorns from her pads, taught him about traps and always and particularly to beware of Shere Khan, who still thirsted for his blood. As for Kaa, the Rock Python, he gave the boy no lessons, but he delighted to play with him and would wind himself up in great shimmering coils, fold upon fold, and let the boy rest his head and his back among them when he was weary.

Not only the gray wolf-cubs but all these friends called him Little Brother, and Akela, Leader of the Pack, told him plainly that he should depend on him to defend him when he grew old and toothless.

Bagheera it was, with his experience of men and in Kings' Palaces, who first told Mowgli that he was not a Wolf and never would be one however old he grew, and that when he was older he would surely be led back to his people as he, Bagheera, had been led back to the Jungle. Mowgli sulked at first when he heard this talk but he listened when Bagheera told of what he had heard of Shere Khan's plots to destroy him. "Thou wilt never live to be a man, Little Brother," cautioned Bagheera, "except thou first slay the Lame Tiger. And I have a thought concerning this. Canst thou secure some of the Red Flower that grows by men's huts at night, for of this all beasts are afraid, even I who speak, and with this thou canst defend Akela and even slay Shere Khan, perchance."

Now Mowgli knew that by the Red Flower, fire was meant. He had seen it glowing in earthen pots as he peered into the village and knew that men fed it with leaves and twigs and branches that it should not die. That very night he stole softly to the huts, saw where the Red Flower was blooming, caught up a pot when none were looking, bore it away to the rocks and fed and tended it throughout the night and day. As he bent above it he thought many times of the hut through whose windows he had glanced and of some one there with soft voice and gentle hands who perhaps might be a Mother such as Bagheera had told him about and his heart felt a stirring to return and look at her.

But first Akela must be defended, for Mowgli heard that next night a Council should be held to depose the old wolf as Leader and the man-cub must be there to fight the Pack with the Red Flower and if need be to show Shere Khan who was Master, with a bit of that same blossom.

All came off as had been foretold at the Council meeting. Akela was tried, pronounced old and toothless, and was about to be deposed when Mowgli arose, defended his old friend with passion, cried out against the ingratitude of the Pack and waving a blazing branch which he had lighted from the pot, so affrighted the Wolves that the most part swiftly changed their minds and fawned upon their Leader. The little Frog even threatened to thrust the branch down Shere Khan's throat if he did not leave the Council immediately, and the great Tiger, breathing dire vengeance, turned tail and slunk, growling, to his lair.

But now all the beasts recognized by these things that Mowgli had become a man with a man's strength and courage and they told him, with bitter sorrow, that it was no more fit that he should live among them. Those among the Wolves who would have deposed and killed Akela and those whose fur had been singed with the sparks from the burning branch, ran from the Council and soon but a few, with Father and Mother Wolf, the four Gray Brothers, Akela, Baloo and Bagheera, were left beside the little Frog.

Then something began to hurt inside him as he had never been hurt before and he sobbed and the tears ran down his face.

"What is this?" he said. "I do not wish to leave the Jungle and I do not know what this is. Am I dying, Bagheera?"

"Those are but tears that only men use," said Bagheera. "Now I know thou art a man and must go back to thy people. Let the tears fall, little Brother: they will not harm thee!"

Then Mowgli said farewell to Mother Wolf as they bade him, and cried on her rough coat while the four Gray Brothers howled miserably and vowed they would never forget him, but the lad's heart was not altogether broken, for he had no real thought of tarrying among his own people, but promised himself he would stay with them just long enough to learn their ways and their talk and would come back when he had learned greater wisdom, with Shere Khan's hide to stretch upon Council Rock.

When night fell Mowgli crept down the hill to the village and greatly daring, drew near the window of the hut where he had glimpsed the Woman with the soft voice. She started and screamed at first when she saw his head in the glow of the cooking-pot, but when he opened his mouth and made signs that he was hungry she beckoned him in and gave him warm milk and little cakes.

Finding him gentle she stroked and patted him and entreated him to stay with her, for long ago she had lost a child who had wandered away and another had never come to take his place. Mowgli understood her gestures, though he did not yet know a word of the language of men, and as he had a purpose in staying, he did as he was bidden and slept beneath her roof, though the close air almost choked him.

He was quick in learning some of the language and many of the ways of men, submitted to the smoothing of his locks and to the wearing of a fragment, at least, of manly garments, and in three months' time was allowed to go beyond the bounds of the village as a herder of the buffaloes.

So he could meet every day one of the Gray Brothers, and indeed they had never deserted him, but had cried him the news every night from the hillside. With their help and Bagheera's he was able to engineer a stampede of the buffalo herd and so at length to compass the death of his old enemy, Shere Khan, in a narrow ravine whence he could not escape. He was able, too, to stretch the Tiger's velvet-striped hide upon the Council Rock as he had vowed, but so much of magic seemed to the head men of the village to lie in his actions and in his strange communications with the jungle beasts that, in spite of the prayers of the Woman who had befriended him, he was driven forth from their midst.

How he went back to the jungle for a time and how he fared there, of his terrible adventure in the Cold Lairs with the monkey-folk, of how Fear came to the forest in the season of Drought—of these you must learn in the two

"Jungle Books," for I have but lifted out of them the thread of Mowgli's story and it is only one among the many shining strands of the weaving.

Swinging in his hammock, knotted of creepers in tall tree-tops fifty feet above the ground, Mowgli used to sing himself to sleep in these days with rhymes of jungle laws and jungle wisdom; but it was none of these but pure love and gratitude that led him to the cave when Father and Mother Wolf lay dying and that prompted him to watch with the Gray Brothers as the old pair departed for the Happy Hunting-grounds.

It was gratitude, too, that led him to deliver the Wolf Pack from the assault of the Wild Dogs; and in gratitude he held the head of Akela, the Lone Wolf, as he perished in this last battle.

"Go to thine own people again," panted Akela, as he lay upon the ground. "Little Brother, wolfling of my watching, go to thine own people: there is thy place."

But Mowgli would not go as yet, nor would he choose a mate in the jungle as his foster-brothers had already done, though bright were their eyes and sleek their coats. He had seen other eyes, dark and tender, glossy braids down-dropping and a face like a jasmine-flower among the maidens of a village far away and of these he dreamed when Spring came again and the Time of New Talk.

Baloo watched him, and knew his trouble; Kaa, the Rock Python, read his thoughts, and Bagheera, skilled in the ways of men, watched him, also. They knew that he must go, and at last one day Baloo said to him, gravely: "Little Frog, go thou now and make thy lair with thine own blood and pack and people. Remember that we love thee and that the Jungle is thine at call." And as the beasts saw their beloved nursling, half-smiling, half-weeping, make his way down the hill toward the distant village, they cried together:

"Good hunting on a new trail, Master of the Jungle."

# LITTLE NELL

AVE you ever walked along the crowded streets of a great city and seen, in some little shop where they sell old furniture, old dishes, and old ornaments, a pink and white Dresden China shepherdess smiling out on you through the dim glass? Just such a pink and white, curling-haired, and dainty figure was Charles Dickens's "Little Nell," and in just such an old curiosity shop did she live with her grandfather—a loving, unselfish, housewifely little Nell, taking as good care of the old man as any woman could have done, and watching over him as if she had been the elder and he an infant in her charge.

The Old Curiosity Shop was in London, in a dark and dingy street. It was a dark and dingy shop, too, where few people came and few people bought, but Nell brightened it like a ray of sunshine on a stormy day.

Darling little Nell, the world's darling ever since Dickens told her story—there is room in these pages for only part of her adventures, for "The Old Curiosity Shop," the book that tells about them, is a long one with a complicated plot and filled with many characters.

Nelly Trent, for that was the whole of Little Nell's name, had no kith or kin in all the land but her grandfather and her good-for-naught brother, Fred; and of Fred she saw very little save when he wanted money. Long days she spent alone in the dusky shop among the curiosities—rusty weapons, suits of armor, grinning idols, bronze dragons, strange stuffed birds. Many nights alone, too, for her grandfather in his efforts to regain the money he had lost had become a confirmed gambler. Not for himself did he borrow money at enormous rates of interest to waste upon the gaming table, but for his beloved little Nell, whom he planned in his disordered mind to "make rich one of these days, and a fine lady."

Most of this money was borrowed from Daniel Quilp, "an uglier dwarf than could be seen anywhere for a penny," with sly, black eyes, grizzled, frowzy black hair, long crooked finger-nails, and his few remaining teeth constantly showing in a wide, malicious grin.

It was to Daniel Quilp's moldy office on a dilapidated wharf that Nelly was often sent to bring back bags of coin for her grandfather; so often, of late, that the suspicious dwarf began to wonder what the old man did with it, and to doubt whether it would be safe to advance any more, even with the security behind him of the shop and its contents.

Learning from the child, by his sly questions, that her grandfather now spent most of his nights away from home and returned in the morning exhausted and falling upon his bed to groan himself to sleep, the cunning dwarf began to have a strong idea as to how his money was spent, and a stronger opinion still that all supplies must henceforth be cut off.

The prospect of a serious loss where great profits had been expected, at once converted the covetous Quilp into a malicious enemy, and now poor Nell had but one friend in all the width of London—good Kit, honest, homely Kit, the shop-boy, with his shock-head, wide mouth, red cheeks, and comical, turned-up nose. He was devoted to his little mistress and to everything she possessed down to her linnet in its battered cage; and after his day's work was over and he ran to his poor home and his widowed mother for his supper, he often hurried back again to keep watch in the street lest anything should happen to "Miss Nell," while her guardian was away. Miss Nell had taught him to write; she had often gone to see his mother, his little brother Jacob and the baby, and she always watched over his comfort and saw that he had a bite to eat when he returned from long, wearisome errands. No wonder he adored her; and no wonder, either, that Quilp hated him and wanted him out of the way, lest he interfere with some of the malicious schemes that the dwarf was working up against the curiosity shop and its master.

On the last occasion that Nell had been sent to the wharf for money, the dwarf had refused it, but had said that he would call at the shop in a few days; and ever since the old man had been half crazed with anxiety, wondering if Quilp would come, wondering what could be done if he did not appear, restless, beating his hands together, crying out that he was ruined, ruined! Poor little Nell, whose strength and courage had weakened during the last year of loneliness and anxiety, and who feared Quilp and his influence upon her grandfather, began to beg him to give up the shop if indeed he were ruined and had nothing more to hope for in London

"Dear grandfather," she cried, "let us leave this sad place tomorrow and beg our way from door to door, if we must. Let us never set foot in dark rooms or melancholy houses any more, but wander up and down wherever we like; and I will beg for both of us," and she clung about his neck and wept upon his shoulder.

The old man wept, too, and their tears so blinded them that they did not see that Quilp had slipped into the room meantime and was quietly listening to what they said. It took but a moment, when they had once seen him, for him to declare no, he had brought no more money; no, he never should bring any more; he had discovered the old man's secret, and knew where his coin had been going; the debt was already more than could ever be paid, even though he took over the entire shop, which he should do, and promptly at that.

Trembling, gasping with the shock of Quilp's words, the old man falteringly asked how his secret had been discovered, and the dwarf answered, maliciously, as being the worst thing he could say, that Kit, the shop-boy, had told him.

Kit had told him—their own Kit in whom they so trusted! He was to be dismissed from that hour; Nell was to pay him and say that they never would look upon his face again, and so saying, her grandfather fell to the floor, unconscious. A doctor was called, the old man laid upon his bed, and, when all was quiet again, poor Nell went weeping to Kit's home, gave him his money and dismissed him. Which was the most grieved and astonished, Kit, his mother, little Jacob, or the baby, it would be hard to tell, especially as Nell sobbed over and over again that she had been bidden not to tell why the boy was henceforth to be banished.

There followed a long illness for the grandfather, during which Quilp, fearing perhaps that he might lose something if he were not on hand, took up his bed and board at the curiosity shop and claimed its contents. As the old man grew stronger in body, it was easy to see that he became more feeble in mind, and now every day when they could be sure of not being overheard, Nell urged that they should leave their miserable life and the miserable house, no longer their own. She had no one to whom she could appeal for advice on this or any other subject, for Kit must not be spoken to, and her good-for-naught brother had not been seen for months, nor did they know his whereabouts.

It was true that Nell was fourteen years old; but her parents had died soon after her birth, she had been brought up by an old man whose troubles had quite unhinged his mind, and she had lived all her life in the little shop and knew no more of the world than her linnet in its cage. Innocent and inexperienced as she was, she dreamed only of freeing herself and her grandfather from Quilp and his wicked schemes, and of escaping to fresh air and sunshine from the dark corner where they lived. She thought of the country as a kind of heaven, where everybody was free and happy. She had saved a little money, and when it was gone she would work for more, and beg, if need be.

Her grandfather, now quite childish, easily agreed to her plans, and very early one fine morning they slipped away from the old shop, leaving Quilp snoring on Nell's little bed, which he had appropriated for his own use. Neither of the fugitives had the least idea of where to go when they had once escaped. They had no plans, no destination in mind, but they hurried away from the noisy streets and were delighted when at last they reached a quiet green roadside where they could eat their scanty breakfast.

It may be thought that in the days that followed some one would have noticed them and asked their business and whither they were traveling; but in Great Britain it is not at all unusual to see men, women, and children too, walking along the roads with bundles upon their backs. They may be tramps, or gypsies, or tinkers, or sturdy farm laborers on their way to new employment; but they are no cause for astonishment and create no especial interest.

As raindrops on a stormy day slide down the windowpane and run together into a pool upon the sill, so Nell and her grandfather slid into the quiet pool of the countryside, which received them as quietly. Kit, who, in spite of his dismissal, frequently hung about the shop to inquire how his old master and his little mistress were faring, happened there on the very day of their flight and was kicked and beaten furiously by Quilp, who insisted that the boy knew where they had gone. Kit endured this punishment as patiently as he could, not only because he thought he might thus learn something more of the matter from the dwarf, but because he wanted to secure Nell's bird, which hung in its old place. The cage once under his arm, the lad ran home with it, sobbing all the way, not because of the beating, but because dear Miss Nell had gone, and gone without a word to him.

Nell and her grandfather trudged along all that day—sleeping at night in a wayside cottage where were beds to let—and all the next day too, although that afternoon a kindly carrier picked them up and gave them a corner in his cart. The old man constantly begged that they should go "further away, dear Nell, further away," and seemed to have a constant dread that Quilp would pursue them, though what more he could get from them, having already taken all, it would have been hard to say.

The carrier set them down in a village where he supposed they had intended to go, and, wandering about, looking for a night's lodging, they came upon a Punch and Judy show which was being put to rights in a deserted churchyard. The old man was attracted at once and begged to stay and see what was going on; and as Nell offered to patch Judy's tattered dress and furbish up Punch's hat, they were welcomed and advised to walk on with the proprietors that night to the race-course, where were to be great doings on the morrow.

Short, a red-faced, merry-eyed man, was exceedingly cordial as they walked along; but Codlin, a surly sort of fellow, often eyed their new companions slyly and told his partner that night that he'd wager that child was missed where she came from, and that somebody would be offering good money to them as would find her, before long.

As they came nearer and nearer to the fair grounds, they found the roads filled with strange folks; men and women traveling on stilts; giants, almost as tall as the stilt-walkers; dwarfs, much smaller than Quilp and much more attractive; and a company of performing dogs with red blankets on their backs and little red caps on their dusty heads. Had the child not been hungry, weary, and full of care, all these sights would have delighted her;

but she thought only of the fact that their money was now almost gone, and that tomorrow begging must begin. They slept in a corner of a tent that night, and next day Nell was able to make up a few bunches of wild flowers and to sell them here and there; but both she and her grandfather had now become aware of Codlin's suspicious looks, and determined to leave the Punch and Judy show as soon as an opportunity offered.

About noontime, when the noise and gayety of the races and the side-shows were at their height, the unhappy pair seized upon the right moment, crept out of sight, and made their way to the open fields again. By this time the old man had begun to realize that his mind was going, and was possessed by a fear that he would be dragged away from Nell and taken to an asylum; so he constantly urged the frail child to greater speed upon their way. All that afternoon they hurried along over woodland paths, and toward night came to a tiny village where men and boys were playing cricket on the green. Seeking a shelter for the night, they came to a school whose master sat reading on the porch, and they timidly asked him for a lodging. He gladly took them in, kept them over the next day, and would have had them stay longer, for he loved children and his heart yearned over little Nell with her pale cheeks, travel-stained dress, and worn shoes.

But grandfather was restless and feared pursuit, and they bade adieu to the kind schoolmaster and traveled on again, coming next day, fortunately, upon an unexpected situation and a new friend. Drawn up by the wayside, as they walked, they saw a neatly painted caravan, two horses grazing near by, and a stout lady seated upon its steps comfortably taking her tea. She noted quickly little Nell's pallor and her limping gait, and offered a cup to the travelers, talking with them meantime, and growing more and more attracted toward the delicate child with her lovely, anxious face. She finally asked the pair into the caravan, and promised them conveyance to the next town where she was to display her wax figures—Mrs. Jarley's wax figures—she being Mrs. Jarley, "the delight of the nobility and gentry, and the peculiar pet of the royal family." The three travelers made friends so swiftly on the trip that before its end the impetuous lady had offered a post as assistant in the wax-work show to little Nell, who accepted it with unbounded gratitude, for here at last she might rest awhile and lay down the burden of care which had grown too heavy for her failing strength.

If only the poor child, so frail and feeble now, might have stayed with Mrs. Jarley and her wonderful wax figures, might have discharged her simple duties and felt a motherly care about her the while; but it was not to be, for the old man soon fell in with evil companions in the town, began to gamble again, and must be taken away from them at once, lest worse ills befall.

So with broken heart the suffering child again took up her load of care, escaped from the caravan by night, and fared forth with her charge, she knew not whither. Nature herself seemed against them now, for rain fell, winds blew, and once the warm ashes beside a factory furnace had to serve as their couch and their bedding for the night. Nell felt every day that she grew weaker and could not long protect her grandfather, but what was to become of him without her, friendless and feeble as he was?

At the very moment when she was about to give way altogether, Heaven sent a friend, for they met the schoolmaster again, traveling along their road toward a new and better appointment in a distant village. Running to his side, Nell begged his aid for herself and the old man, and looking up into his kindly face with streaming eyes, she fainted in his arms.

The good man carried her to an inn near by, made her comfortable in bed, and when she was refreshed begged her to tell him all her story. This the child thankfully did, and, calling the bewildered and distressed grandfather to the bedside, the schoolmaster offered to take them both with him to his new position and there to find them food and shelter.

Meantime, search for the fugitives was going on everywhere, in every way, with no success. Nell's uncle, long a resident of foreign lands, had suddenly returned to England to find his only relatives missing and their property in the hands of Quilp. No one knew where they had gone, and repeated inquiries of the few who had known them brought no result. By and by rumors came in that a Punch and Judy Show had met them on a race-track; and the uncle, after long search, at last found Codlin and Short, who could only report that they had certainly seen the pair, but long had lost them. Another wild-goose chase was for Mrs. Jarley's Wax-work Show, but "the pet of the royal family" knew nothing save that she herself was seeking Nell.

At last news came from the distant village where the good schoolmaster had conveyed the poor wanderers; but although he had found them shelter and employment, it had been all too late for little Nell. The uncle, taking Kit with him as an earnest of good-will, posted off at once to rescue and comfort the child and her grandfather; but she could tarry no longer in the unfriendly world and before they could arrive, her tired heart had ceased to beat.

They found her calm and beautiful in her white robes, her couch decked with green leaves and winter berries and her grandfather weeping by her side. Life had been too hard for her gentle spirit; but she slept a happy sleep, and we know that her waking was "happier than tongue can tell or heart of man conceive."

# REBECCA OF SUNNYBROOK FARM

IF you have ever been so fortunate as to meet Rebecca Rowena Randall of Sunnybrook Farm, either in the book that bears her name, in the second volume, "New Chronicles of Rebecca," in the play, or in the moving picture, you will recall her as a spirited and adventurous young person with brilliant dark eyes, two long dark braids of hair, a stiffly starched buff calico frock, and a precious pink parasol.

Just this she was when she stepped down from the old stage-coach at Aunt Miranda's door in Riverboro; just so she looked when she drove into her author's dream one night, attended by the rattle of wheels and the trot, trot of horses' hoofs—for Kate Douglas Wiggin tells us that she was, in reality, a dream-child like "Alice in Wonderland." She seems to have had the dream faculty, too, of transforming herself into many different shapes, for she has already, in the years since her birth, appeared in Swedish, Norwegian, Danish, Dutch, Polish, German, Bohemian, Roumanian, and Italian guises.

Here are some of her names in foreign tongues:

Rebecca von Sonnenbach Hof,

Rebeka ze Stonecznego Potoku,

Rebekka fra Solbaek gaarden,

Rebecca van Zonbeek-Hoeve.

She still remains, however, wherever she travels, "the nicest child in American literature," as Thomas Bailey Aldrich called her; but it is not because she is an ideal human creature, but because she is a real little girl, with all a girl's faults and follies.

Rebecca Rowena, "named out of 'Ivanhoe,'" as she tells us, was one of seven children who lived a happy-go-lucky life on Sunnybrook Farm, "way off from everywhere." Their widowed mother was too overburdened with work to give careful supervision to each child, and it may be said, in general, that Hannah looked after Rebecca more or less, both of them after John and Jenny, and all four of them after Mark, Fanny, and Mira. Life had to be made very simple if it were to be lived at all with such a family; and when Aunt Miranda asked Rebecca, soon after she came to Riverboro, if she hadn't put her dress on "hind-side foremost," Rebecca quickly answered: "No; that's all right. If you have seven children, you can't keep buttonin' 'em and unbuttonin' 'em all the time—they have to do themselves. We're always buttoned up in front at our house."

At Sunnybrook Farm, where Aurelia Randall, Rebecca's mother, lived, was poverty and seven children to share it. In the Brick House at River-boro, where the maiden aunts, Jane and Miranda, resided, was a comfortable income and no children at all, so, of course, the sensible thing to do was to try to balance the situation more evenly. That was what the aunts thought; and so Hannah, the eldest hope, was invited to come to them to be fed and lodged, clothed and educated, amid the superior advantages of Riverboro. But Hannah was steady and industrious, and greatly needed at home; so it was Rebecca, the little brown elf, the gay, generous, loving, willful, prankish Rebecca, who came to the old aunts.

When her mother put her in the stage, in charge of Uncle Jerry Cobb, on the day of her departure for Riverboro, the child announced that no one need worry about her for she was "used to traveling, she'd been on a journey before—a little one, but it's always a journey when you carry a nightgown," she insisted. The old stage-driver accepted the charge of his youthful passenger and promised to set her down at the right house; but, little knowing her temperament, he expected her to sit quietly inside his vehicle, and he was somewhat startled when, by and by, a small pink parasol stabbed him in the arm and a small voice inquired: "Does it cost any more to ride up there with you? The stage is so much too big for me, that I rattle round in it till I'm most black and blue."

Lifted to the front seat beside the driver, Rebecca smoothed her dress, pushed back her hat, and prepared to enjoy herself, remarking, as an opening for conversation, that it was "a good growing day."

"It is, certain," said Uncle Jerry; "too hot, most. Why don't you put up your parasol?"

"Oh, dear, no!" exclaimed Rebecca. "I never put it up when the sun shines. Pink fades awfully, you know. It's the dearest thing in life to me; but it's an awful care."

At that moment, Mr. Cobb realized, as he told his wife that night, that the bird perched by his side was a bird of very different feather from those to which he was accustomed, but on the whole he must have admired her plumage for they became fast friends on that summer morning, and his home was Rebecca's refuge whenever storms raged at the Brick House.

That there were storms you do not need to be told, when you realize that the aunts were elderly ladies, careful, house-proud, and quite unused to children. Aunt Miranda prophesied, while she was getting ready for Rebecca, that the child wouldn't pick up anything after herself, probably never saw a duster, and would be as hard to train into their ways as if she had been a heathen.

Aunt Jane, whose heart was a trifle softer, did not take quite such a gloomy view of the question; and in her first letter home, Rebecca told her mother that she didn't believe Aunt Jane "hated" her quite as much as Aunt Miranda did.

Though the journey from Sunnybrook Farm was in reality a brief one, it held for Rebecca all the elements of a trip around the world, for it meant a farewell to her mother, to her brothers and sisters, to her birthplace, and an introduction to new housemates and a new home. She stepped from the stage on her arrival, a trembling, excited little creature, equally ready to laugh or to cry, according to her reception; but the unsatisfactory nature of the kisses which greeted her, and the torrent of directions poured out by Miss Miranda when she escorted her to her room, as to shutting doors tight, keeping out flies, wiping her feet on the mat, and always using the back stairs, would have daunted the most hopeful child. It is no wonder, when left alone with injunctions to wash her face and hands and brush her hair, that Rebecca stood perfectly still for a moment, and then leaped into the middle of the bed and drew the counterpane up over her head. It showed a desire to escape from a world that was too much for her; but it certainly was a strange proceeding, and you can believe that Aunt Miranda thought it so when she came upstairs to see what was delaying the child.

Although it was long before the elder Aunt found Rebecca anything but a care and a trial, Aunt Jane speedily began to love her; and then her friendship with her neighbor, Emma Jane Perkins, a "rich blacksmith's daughter," came to sweeten daily living. Emma Jane was pink, fair, blue-eyed, plump, rather dull and quiet, but affectionate and loyal to the backbone, and in spite of the contrast between them, or because of it, the two girls were as devoted as a pair of doves. They went to school together, shared each other's joys and sorrows, and, secure in their double strength, extended their protection to a certain Clara Belle Simpson whose neglected brothers and sisters, dilapidated house, and father of doubtful honesty, had not commended her to the other children.

Rebecca soon showed herself a good scholar, was apt at "speaking pieces," at compositions, and even at verse-making, a talent which she had exercised as soon as she could write. It was on a gala afternoon at school when there were to be dialogues, songs, and recitations, that the first heavy storm at the Brick House broke over her devoted head. Rebecca hurried home at noon, meaning to ask if she might wear her new pink gingham for the exercises, but found that the aunts had unexpectedly gone to drive with a neighbor and had left a note explaining the matter. The new dress, just finished by Aunt Jane, lay on her bed; so what wonder that the excited and excitable child hurriedly put it on, found a pink ribbon for her hair, a pink rose for her belt, caught up the pink sunshade, and sped to the schoolhouse to take her part in the wonderful program.

But ah, poor little Rebecca! She had gone up the front stairs to her room, in her haste, dropping her handkerchief on the way as an evidence of guilt; she had left the screen out of her window; she had not cleared away her lunch; and, worst sin of all, she had left the side door unlocked all the afternoon! Add to these things that she had worn the new pink frock without leave, and nobody need be surprised that the aunts, coming home hot and tired, felt as if their charge had broken the entire Ten Commandments with one crash! A storm was brewing without as well as within the house, and amid the muttering of thunder and the flashes of distant lightning, Rebecca was confronted with her crimes, told to go upstairs, put on her nightgown and go to bed, and not let a word be heard from her till next morning.

As the sobbing and rebellious child slipped off the pink frock, a faded rose fell from her belt, and as she stooped to pick it up, she cried to herself: "Spoiled! Just like my happy day!" She was misunderstood and ill-treated, she thought; she would not stay another hour in Riverboro; she would go back to Sunnybrook Farm; Uncle Jerry Cobb should take her on the stage in the morning; she would run away from the Brick House that very minute, for, with the thunder-storm just then in full force, no one would hear her.

Hastily making up a bundle with her nightgown, comb, and toothbrush, she dropped it from the window, slipped out on the roof of the L, caught hold of the lightning-rod, slid down to the porch roof, used the woodbine trellis for a ladder, and flew up the road in the storm.

Uncle Jerry was alone in his kitchen, for Mrs. Cobb was nursing a sick neighbor, and he stood transfixed with surprise when the dripping Rebecca entered. It was clear enough that a tragedy had happened at the Brick House, and he heard the child's story through her sobs, and could not help but sympathize, though he was cautious in expressing himself. It was plain that his "little lady passenger" had been careless and thoughtless, but nothing worse could be said of her; and he soothed her, shared with her his tomato preserve, apple pie, and hot tea, and discussed the whole situation as it looked to him. Oh, yes, of course the stage could set her on her way in the morning; oh, no, no matter about the fare for the present; her mother would approve of her return, no doubt, and there would be no trouble.

At this point, a tiny doubt entered the child's mind, for she was calming down under Uncle Jerry's kindly sympathy. Would her mother approve? Would the aunts be willing to take another of the children in her place? Did she really want to go back to the Farm and be another burden on the family? Ought she not to remember the advantages the aunts were giving her, and ought she not to pay for them by good behavior?

Uncle Jerry noted her hesitation, and craftily remarked that he had been thinking of going over to the Brick House on an errand after supper anyway; and, if she thought best, she might curl up in the corner beside him and slip upstairs the way she had slipped out. "You haven't run away, yet, you know," said he; "so you ain't committed no sin, and when you've had a good night's sleep, you can tell your Aunt Jane all about it, and she'll advise you when to tell Mirandy."

It was good advice, given and taken at the right time, and the storm so cleared the air on both sides that from that day misunderstandings were less frequent and real love began to build its rainbow bridges between the three hearts at the Brick House.

There was a time, a few months later, when Rebecca, feeling that she needed discipline for some offense, resolved to punish herself by throwing her adored pink parasol into the well, as the heathen mothers are supposed to throw their infants, in a spirit of sacrifice, into the Ganges. This step resulted in the catching of the parasol-handle in the chain-gear of the pump, the stoppage of the water supply, and the prolonged services of a man to clear up the difficulty; but even this trial Miranda bore with calmness, remarking, however, that if in future her niece should feel that she needed punishment, the aunts might perhaps be trusted to invent something for her that wouldn't punish the whole family.

Rebecca and Emma Jane Perkins continued their devoted friendship through all these trials, and still watched over the fortunes of Clara Belle Simpson. Thrilled by the Simpsons' plan of selling soap, in order to obtain for their family a certain "banquet lamp" offered as a premium, the two friends entered upon a mercantile career whenever they were allowed to go out together. Rebecca outlined the route and coached Emma Jane as to the proper things to say; but it was she, herself, who secured the wonderful order for three hundred cakes from a strange young man whom she found sitting alone on a cottage piazza, husking corn. When the advantages of this soap—the "Rose-red, Snow-white Brand"—had been enumerated, when it had been explained that Rebecca was engaged in soap-selling because of the great yearning of her poor friends, the Simpsons, for a banquet lamp, the stranger at once gave the above astonishing order, so astonishing that it knocked the excitable Rebecca right over into a clump of lilac bushes!

So entered Adam Ladd, whom, because of the lamp, Rebecca always called "Mr. Aladdin," into her story, and a firm friend he remained through life. When her rustic school-days were past, when, with Emma Jane, she went with incredible pride and dignity to Wareham Female Seminary, when she became editor of the "Wareham School Pilot," when her verses and compositions received public commendation, when she was elected president of her class—in all these things Mr. Aladdin exulted—and so did the aunts in Riverboro.

Rebecca's education had not been accomplished without great sacrifices on their part, for they had lost money and found it hard to make expenses meet, and Aunt Miranda had visibly weakened and grown old under the experience. In the meantime nothing was going well at the Farm, which had long been mortgaged, and it seemed even doubtful if the interest money for the year could be raised. It was then that Mr. Aladdin "rubbed his lamp" and offered a fifty-dollar composition prize at the Seminary, hoping, of course, that Rebecca might gain it, which, equally of course, she did, though she could apply it to nothing more romantic than paying the interest on "that detestable mortgage."

The wonderful day of Rebecca's graduation came at last, when Mr. Aladdin and old Uncle Jerry watched a hay-cart wreathed with daisies rumble down the village street, saw the white-clad girls of the class grouped within it, the boys marching by its side, and in front, seated on a green-covered bench like a throne, their Rebecca, "their prodigy and pearl." Uncle Jerry nearly wore out the pew he sat in during the exercises that followed by his stamping and applause, and when Rebecca recited her class poem, "Makers of Tomorrow," his approval was so marked as to draw all eyes in his direction. Rebecca, however, had noted from the beginning of the exercises that the aunts were not present, and heard and saw through a mist until she learned that Aunt Miranda was very ill and that Aunt Jane could not leave her.

Her flight was swift, then, back to the Brick House. She folded up and laid away her graduation dress that night, yearning to be of service in what she soon knew would be her old aunt's last days. Mr. Aladdin stayed near by and rendered every service in his power; but most of all he lightened Rebecca's burdens by assuring her that he had arranged for her mother the sale of Sunnybrook Farm to the new railway company that had long been bargaining for the land. The sum received would be a good one, enough to pay off that leaden-weighted mortgage and yet leave a substantial something for Mrs. Randall and her brood.

There was perplexity in Rebecca's mind even then as to what roof would shelter her family when they should leave the old home; but when Aunt Miranda closed her tired eyes at last, it was found that she had settled that question by willing all that she possessed—house, furniture, and land—to the little niece who had been such a trial to her in her childhood.

No wonder that the girl's heart overflowed with gratitude to the guardian of her youth who had proved to be as kindly and generous in heart as her manner and her tongue had been sharp. The old lady had in truth been the "making" of all that Rebecca was and all she hoped to be, and the girl whispered to herself as she heard what had been done for her: "God bless Aunt Miranda! God bless the Brick House that was! God bless the Brick House that is to be!"

**THE END**